M000085516

Reflection:
Thorn of the White Rose

Records of the Ohanzee Book 3

Rachel R. Smith

Text Copyright © 2016 Rachel R. Smith

Cover Image by West Coast Design

All rights reserved. No part of this publication may be reproduced,
distributed, or transmitted in any form or by any means, including
photocopying, recording, or other electronic or mechanical methods,
without the prior written permission of the publisher, except in the
case of brief quotations embodied in critical reviews and certain other
noncommercial uses permitted by copyright law.

This is a work of fiction. All characters, places, and events are
imaginary. Any resemblance to actual persons, living or dead, or
actual events is purely coincidental.

ISBN 978-0-9963892-5-9

DEDICATION

To my dad, lunch buddy and ever-patient mapmaker.

And to my mamaw, much love from your favorite
granddaughter (albeit the only one).

CONTENTS

1

INK, PAPER, AND A SECRET MEETING

Charis

Charis picked up the last book from the table in front of her and flipped it open, fanning the pages as she inhaled the heavenly aroma of fresh ink and paper. The pleasantness of the scent was further enhanced by the fact that this book was the very last one from—what had been—two towering stacks of new acquisitions she catalogued and processed this evening. Her left hand ached from hours of carefully recording each book's information into the log and copying the relevant details onto cards for the University Library's card catalog. She wasn't even supposed to be working tonight. But, when half of the staff had been too sick to report to work, Charis volunteered to take on an extra shift at the last minute. It seemed like everyone was getting sick lately.

As if summoned by her thought, there came a sneeze followed by a sniffle from the woman sitting beside her.

"It sounds like you're getting sick too. Are you sure you don't want to go home and rest?" Charis asked the Head

Librarian. "I can finish the remainder of this by myself."

"I can rest—," the woman began, pausing midsentence to wrinkle her nose and hold up one finger while she tugged a handkerchief from her pocket with a free hand. She blew into the cloth, emitting a painful-sounding honk before speaking again. "I can rest when the work is finished."

Charis winced, partially in sympathy and partially out of concern for her own health. "Well, if you insist on staying, at least we're almost done."

The Head Librarian managed a thin smile. "I do appreciate your help this evening. It's a shame that more of your coworkers don't share your dedication. How silly to let something like a little cold keep them from coming in."

Charis accepted the woman's compliment with a smile, though she wasn't sure that she would have reported in either if she weren't feeling well. It was important to be reliable and to take pride in your work, but there was such a thing as being too committed—and the Head Librarian was a prime example of that. At the very moment that thought crossed Charis' mind, the woman's hand flew up to her mouth to muffle her next cough. It was a good thing she did since it may otherwise have drowned out the soft knocking that came from the doorway at the same time.

"Good evening, ladies," Charis' father called out. "I thought I'd drop by to let you know that my meeting in the Special Collection Room has wrapped up. Amon should be leaving shortly as well."

"Thank you," the Head Librarian replied. "I take it Amon will lock the room on his way out?" Her tone made it clear that the last part was more of an instruction than a question. "The gate was left open a few weeks ago. Even though it didn't cause a problem, I don't want it to become a habit."

Charis squirmed in her seat as she fought to maintain a neutral expression. It was her fault that the gate had been left open on the night of the Arts Festival. Well, not entirely my fault, she silently amended. Amon moving the ladder and stranding her in the window nook had made her so angry and flustered that she stormed out without even thinking about the gate. In her opinion, that made him responsible too.

"I reminded him to lock up before leaving," Charis' father affirmed before turning his attention to Charis. "I didn't expect to see you here. I thought you were off tonight."

"I was supposed to be, but I offered to come in since so many of the staff are sick."

"And she's done the work of three this evening," the Head Librarian added.

"I would expect no less." His voice was stern, but a ghost of a smile flittered across his lips as he spoke. "Will you be done soon? I can wait and walk home with you."

"Go on, Charis dear. I can handle what's left," the Head Librarian said while attempting to stifle another sneeze.

Charis shook her head firmly. "There's no need for you to wait," she said to her father. "I want to help with a few final tasks, so I'll be here awhile."

A look of understanding crossed her father's face. "In that case, I won't distract you anymore. Don't be out too late," he said before departing.

Charis spent the next half hour sorting each of the newly catalogued books onto carts based on the section of the library where they would be shelved. The Head Librarian stubbornly persisted with her own work, alternately sniffling, sneezing, and coughing all the while.

Finally, just as Charis was about to push the first cart out of the room, the older woman laid down her pen with a sigh and looked up at the clock. "I think I've done as much as I can for tonight. It's nearly time for curfew anyway."

The thought of King Casimer's curfew still made Charis bristle, but she refrained from voicing her disapproval. Instead, she said, "It will take me a few minutes to deliver all these carts to the circulation desks. Please go on home. There's no need for you to wait for me."

"That's very considerate of you, dear," the woman said as she wrapped a fur-lined cape around her shoulders in preparation to leave. "I'm sure I'll be feeling much better in the morning."

"I'm sure you will," Charis agreed, even though she doubted that would be the case. She bid the Head Librarian goodnight and then pushed the cart down a short hallway and into the body of the library.

Shadows loomed out from the towering shelves, crisscrossing with one another to form a pattern of patches in varying degrees of blackness that almost seemed to imitate the room's checkerboard floor. Not a single glow lamp hung from the chandeliers or wall sconces. They had all been removed by the day staff hours ago when the library closed and been taken to the racks outside to recharge in tomorrow's sunlight. Although the moonlight barely provided enough light to see, the darkness didn't bother Charis. She had worked late many times, and she knew the library well enough to navigate through the numerous rows and aisles with her eyes closed.

The first few cart deliveries were completed quickly and uneventfully. Unfortunately, that trend did not persist for long. The fourth cart had a squeaky wheel that filled the silent library with its constant, echoing screech, leaving Charis with a ringing in her ears afterward. The fifth cart, much to her dismay, was also in dire need of repair. One of the wheels fluttered back and forth, making contact with the floor at random intervals. Whenever it did, the cart would lurch unpredictably in one direction or another. It took every ounce of her strength to keep it from careening into the bookcases on either side of the narrow aisle. Charis seethed with irritation as the cart nearly escaped from her grasp yet again. Never before had the walk to the fiction section seemed quite so long. By the time she reached the desk, she wanted nothing more than to give the cart a frustrated shove and walk away. The only thing preventing her from doing so was the fear that it would topple over in the process, and then she would have to pick up all the books. Instead, she gently brought the cart to a stop beside the desk, pivoted on one heel, and flounced away.

As she made her way back down the central aisle for the last cart, a reverberating thud rang out. Though loud, the sound wasn't entirely unexpected. Noises made in the spacious entryway area had a tendency to carry throughout the building—especially when it was empty. Charis assumed this one had been made by the doors closing behind either Amon or the Head Librarian on their way out.

Sure enough, Charis returned to find a darkened office. The Head Librarian had taken all but one of the glow lamps from this room out to the racks before leaving. Charis was glad that the woman hadn't decided to wait for her. She really wasn't in the mood to make the obligatory small talk on the way home.

There was no sense in coming back to the office, so she slid her arms into the straps of her backpack, put on her cape, and shuttered the remaining glow lamp. She muttered a quick prayer that the last cart would be more cooperative since it was bound for the reference desk on the opposite side of the library.

To Charis' great relief, the last cart had none of the quirks the previous two possessed. It glided down the aisles silently and effortlessly as if the weight of the books it carried was no burden at all. This was a fortunate stroke of luck since the other carts would have been too loud or too distracting for Charis to notice the distant, but distinct, rattle of Amon closing the gate to the Special Collection Room.

Keep quiet, Charis, she told herself. Like her father, Amon didn't know she had volunteered to work tonight. If he did discover she was still here, particularly this close to curfew, she was sure he would insist on walking home together. Given a choice, she would rather have left with the Head Librarian. At least around her, Charis' mind didn't turn into a befuddling jumble of emotions.

She didn't want to attract Amon's attention, so once she brought the cart to a halt beside the reference desk, she slipped off her shoes. If Amon was leaving the Special Collection Room, he was much closer to the main entrance than she was. There was no need for Charis to hurry. All she needed to do was stay out of sight and wait for him to leave. She moved furtively toward the front of the building, peeking around the corners of bookcases for any sign of Amon before tiptoeing across the aisles between them. Her ears strained in eager anticipation for the thundering of the doors to signal his departure.

Her maneuver was proceeding smoothly until Amon stepped into sight at the opposite end of the row of bookshelves, striding purposefully away from the entrance. Charis jerked her head back into the safety of the shadows and pressed herself against the endcap. Staring up at the ceiling, she held in a vexed sigh. He must have forgotten something in the Special Collection Room. Why else would he be coming this way?

Charis considered making a dash for the entryway. After all, she was already wearing her pack and cape. If she moved quickly enough, she could be out and on her way home before he reemerged from the Special Collection Room. But if Amon somehow happened to spot her, she would never be able to come up with a reasonable explanation for why she was scurrying through the dark library in her socks. She supposed it would be more sensible to give up and call out to him, but when it came to Amon, her stubbornness frequently won out over sensibility.

Making an uncharacteristically impulsive decision, Charis followed him. She couldn't risk having him come up on her from behind, so there was no other choice but to keep her eyes on him. Surprisingly, he passed the arched hallway leading to the Special Collection Room without hesitation and continued along the exterior wall until he reached an unmarked door. He reached into his pocket to withdraw a key, and Charis' shoulders relaxed. She didn't know why he was using the side door, but at this point, she didn't care.

Her respite was short-lived, however. Instead of leaving, Amon stepped aside, allowing a tall man with a long ponytail to come in. Charis' eyes widened in recognition. Though the man was wearing a floor-length cloak, it was pushed aside so that the sword at his hip was on full display. His hair, coupled with the sword and his commanding stance, immediately reminded Charis of Nerissa's companion, Raysel. Was Amon meeting with Nerissa's allies?

A mixture of astonishment and guilt washed over her. Nerissa herself had warned that knowledge of the Ohanzee was a closely guarded secret—people's lives depended on that secrecy. Suddenly, she saw Amon's suspicious past behaviors in an entirely different light. Hadn't he tried to reassure her that he wasn't really as bad as she made him out to be? Of course he couldn't tell her he was involved with the Ohanzee. All this time he had been helping Nerissa's allies, and all she had done was return his attempts at kindness with nothing but suspicion and hostility.

The two men exchanged words briefly, but Charis was too far away to overhear their quiet conversation. Now feeling far too curious to stay put and emboldened by the presence of one of the Ohanzee, she slunk down the aisle toward them, careful to keep the bookcase between her and their line of sight. This had the unfortunate side effect of also obscuring her view. She crouched down, skimming the shelves until she found a cluster of short books grouped together on both sides of the bookcase. The gap between their tops and the shelf above allowed barely enough room for her to see through.

"Are you certain that we are alone?" the man asked. "I thought I heard something just now."

Charis' eyebrows climbed her forehead as the man looked over his shoulder and stared directly at her hiding spot. She concentrated on holding herself perfectly still, the tip her nose pressing against the spine of one of the books. The whole area was in shadow, and the gap in the shelves was barely taller than her eyes. There was no way he could see her…was there?

"Yes, I'm certain," Amon replied patiently. "I heard the Head Librarian pushing carts around earlier, so I checked her office immediately before coming here to be doubly sure she had gone home. This old building creaks and groans constantly, but those noises are only noticeable at night."

That wasn't the Head Librarian pushing the carts—that was me, Charis corrected silently.

The explanation seemed to satisfy his companion, and the man focused his attention on Amon once more. "You have kept me waiting for too long," he complained.

Amon folded his arms across his chest, and Charis noticed for the first time that he was carrying with him a black leather portfolio. "It couldn't be helped. You were the one who insisted we meet tonight instead of our usual night. This was the earliest I could slip away without the chance of being seen."

"As you say, it couldn't be helped. My schedule is unusually tight right now. I've had to take on a number of additional tasks recently."

"Have your comrades started coming down with the sickness that is going around?" Amon asked.

The man's ponytail swished as he shook his head. "No, only a few have become ill, but our numbers are spread thin. Many have been reassigned to monitor the spread of the outbreak, while others have been assigned to assist with the distribution of experimental medicines and the collection of

Rachel R. Smith

results. Still others have been sent to Silvus and Rhea to deal with a situation…"

He trailed off as a distant rattle rang out, followed by the unmistakable thud of the entryway doors. Charis froze, even as her heartbeat doubled its pace. Though she didn't fear that the Ohanzee man would harm her, she definitely didn't want to be caught. Before she could consider whether to stay in place or run, the man stepped swiftly out the side door. For a fleeting moment, Amon hesitated, his gaze swinging indecisively between where the man had been standing and the front of the library. With a grumble, he spun and hastened toward the source of the sound.

The soft tapping of his footsteps gradually faded away, leaving Charis with nothing but the sound of her own rapid breathing for company. Her knees threatened to give out on her, aching as much from crouching as from nerves. Deciding it would be safe to stay here for now, she eased to the floor, and her legs tingled as the muscles loosened.

A few minutes later, she heard the echo of the main entrance doors closing, followed soon after by more footsteps. They grew louder with every passing second, signaling Amon's return. She rose to her knees and peered through the gap in time to see the man step inside.

"The Head Librarian came back for her lunchbox," Amon said with a hint of annoyance in his voice. "I told her I was finishing up and walked her back to the entrance."

"We will not meet like this again. It's too risky." The man's tone was so low it almost sounded like a growl.

"You are the one who insisted we meet tonight," Amon said, utterly unfazed by the unspoken threat in his companion's

10

tone.

The man grunted in response, but he didn't argue. "Let's get this done so I can be on my way. King Casimer is eager to receive the latest update on your research for him. He thinks he has located the original of one of the paintings described in your notes, but he doesn't want to acquire such a high-value piece without being sure it's the right one."

Charis' chest tightened in an instant, and her heart climbed into her throat as that one statement made the actual truth of the situation readily apparent. This man wasn't one of the Ohanzee. He worked for King Casimer. You should have known better than to think Amon might be an ally, she berated herself. He's been doing research for Casimer on the side all along.

But what did Casimer hope to gain? There would be no reason to hide the fact that he was doing research if the paintings he sought were simply wall decorations—even very valuable ones. Although Marisianne culture focused primarily on science and technology, they also had records on the arts and art history. However, since the University Library contained the most extensive records of artists and their works in all of Renatus, the paintings Casimer was looking for information about must be old and obscure.

Amon unwound the strap that bound the black leather folder in his hands and withdrew a sheaf of papers. "Somehow I doubt the price of any painting is high enough to give my uncle pause," he commented as he handed them over. "Even if he bought the wrong one, the cost would be pocket change for the Treasury of Marise."

The man rolled the papers and secured them within a

tube that he pulled from the lining of his cloak. "Indeed, but even the deepest coffers will empty if the contents are spent frivolously."

"I suppose he is also concerned that it would look bad in the eyes of the public to be buying expensive pieces of artwork while this strange sickness spreads unchecked," Amon relented. "I hope my most recent translations will help him come to a conclusion about that particular painting."

The man nodded in agreement. "We'll meet next on our regular night." Without waiting for a response from Amon, he opened the door and disappeared into the night amidst a swirl of black fabric.

Now that Casimer's messenger was gone, Charis inwardly breathed a sigh of relief. She watched from her hiding spot as Amon locked the side door and then began to walk toward the main entrance of the library. After waiting a few minutes to put some distance between them, she crept down the hallway, dodging from the shadow of one bookcase to the next. This time, Amon did not double back. He went directly to the front doors, and the key jangled as he locked them behind him.

Charis hovered near one of the windows, watching until his retreating form was out of sight before letting herself out as well. If she hurried, she would just have time to get home before curfew.

2

BARR

Nerissa

Fog blanketed the foothills north of Rhea's capital city, wrapping the region in a layer so thick it seemed like the clouds themselves had descended from the surrounding summits. With it came an eerie stillness that made Nerissa feel as if the remainder of the world had faded away. The only visible proof it hadn't was the few branches stretching out from the edges of the murk like skeletal hands offering crumbling leaves glazed in dew. No rustling sounds came from within the invisible trees. Not a single bird call could be heard. Though the morning sun was visible, the hazy veil reduced it to little more than a dim white disk in an otherwise featureless sky.

Nerissa finished checking the knot in the last horse's tether and stepped back to make room for Raysel, who was making his way down the picket line with a bag of oats, pausing to fill each of the feed buckets along the way.

Beware of the spirit that protects the book hidden in the cave. The words from the prophecy tumbled, unbidden, through her thoughts once again, sending a prickling wave of gooseflesh down her skin. She rubbed her arms beneath her cloak and sighed in frustration. The ominous line from the prophecy had lingered in the back of her mind ever since the meeting with Governor Alden two days before. She knew it was a warning that *something* awaited them inside the cave, but what? Spirits and ghosts didn't exist outside of stories, so the reference had to be symbolic. That left one question: what did it symbolize?

Raysel straightened after filling the last bucket and pushed back the hood of his cloak. He studied Nerissa's face for a moment and then narrowed his eyes. "You're worrying about the warning from the prophecy, aren't you?"

Nerissa shifted her eyes away from his, staring over his shoulder into the nothingness instead. "We're about to go into an abandoned mine, which is a dangerous thing to do in the first place. It's doubly so when you've been told to beware of something inside, but you don't know *what* you're supposed to be wary of. That's enough to worry anyone." Her eyes swung back to meet his as she added, "But it isn't going to deter me from retrieving the book."

The lines creasing Raysel's forehead softened. "I don't like the uncertainty either," he concurred while folding the empty burlap bag. "It doesn't help that Alden has been dodging our requests for additional details about the book and the cave."

Nerissa's head bobbed in agreement. Alden *had* been strangely reluctant to divulge any information about either topic. The sole response he had given to their repeated inquiries was a message containing a list of suggested equipment, a map with directions to the mine, and a meeting time. Although that did sufficiently address the logistical needs of their venture, it answered none of their questions.

She had believed Alden was sincere during their initial meeting when he said he would explain later why the book was hidden inside the cave. Now, however, a creeping doubt had worked its way into her mind. It wasn't that she suspected he was going to betray them like Brigs. Even if she had begun to doubt his loyalty, the prophecy provided reassurance that Alden was a true ally. Still, true ally or not, he was definitely hiding something.

Nerissa flinched as Raysel's green eyes suddenly came into focus mere inches from her own. She blinked once in confusion, and for a moment, all she could do was meet his gaze with a blank stare. His face took on a look of concern as he drew away from her.

"You didn't hear a word I said, did you?"

"I'm sorry. I wasn't paying attention." Nerissa knew his question was rhetorical, but she answered anyway.

"Since we're finished here, we should rejoin the others," Raysel repeated. His long ponytail swished with each step he took, sending eddies of mist swirling away in either direction with the movement. Nerissa found it comforting to see him wearing his hair in that familiar way again, particularly after so many weeks of tying it at the base of his neck to mimic the current fashion.

"I have an idea about what the 'spirit' inside the cave might be," he said.

"I'm glad one of us does. What is your idea?"

"It's a simple interpretation—almost too simple," Raysel began. "I think it might be a spirit *crystal*."

Nerissa's eyes widened, and she inhaled sharply. The more she considered the possibility, the more plausible it sounded. "It seems so obvious, now that you've said it. I thought that the reference to a spirit was symbolic, so a spirit crystal would make sense. I would certainly prefer to deal with a crystal over any of the...less tangible options." Her hand drifted to the voice-altering choker around her throat as she spoke. If the warning really were referring to some kind of protective crystal, Tao's presence today would have been invaluable.

"And now you're worrying that you don't know enough about crystals to deal with it on your own," Raysel said with a smirk.

"Wipe that smug look off your face," she scolded, but even as she did so, Nerissa had to fight to keep her lips from curling upward. "Just when I think I've really gotten to know you, I find out something new. How long have you been able to read minds?"

"You give me too much credit. Yours is the only mind I can read," he teased. "Or perhaps your thoughts were written all over your face."

Nerissa glowered at him, but her cheek twitched from the effort of hiding her amusement.

"You don't need to fret so much. You won't be going in alone. Rian, Eloc, and I will all be with you," Raysel continued. "I may not have had someone to mentor me like you did, but I've studied the uses of crystals too. When the time comes, we can figure out how to deal with it together."

"That's right," came Rian's disembodied voice from somewhere nearby. "We'll deal with whatever is waiting inside the cave together."

"Ooooooooooooo," Cole wailed in a ghostly impersonation.

Though she could hear the others clearly, all Nerissa could see was a neat line of faint lights glowing in the haze—a row of glow lamps, unshuttered and ready to be used in the cave.

"Ooooooooooooo," Cole howled again once she and Raysel were close enough to see everyone. "The ghost of the cave is going to get you, Caeneus."

Without a second's hesitation, Rian dropped the pack he was filling with supplies and brought the side of his hand down on Cole's forehead in one quick, chopping motion.

"Oooooo—ow!" Cole's howl turned from ghostly to pained. "Hey! That really hurt, Rian!"

Eloc doubled over, laughing so hard that he snorted. "He bonked you!"

"Knock it off, both of you." Even the fog didn't dull the sharpness in Rian's command. "We're preparing for a mission. I'll turn *you* into a ghost if you keep goofing around."

Raysel shot Rian an approving grin. "I think it's important we keep an open mind to all possibilities, but meeting a ghost is one I feel comfortable ruling out. Ghosts only exist in stories—unless you count that future one," he said while pointing at Cole, who was still rubbing his head and glaring sullenly at Rian.

It was a wasted effort, however. Rian resumed packing the bags with supplies, utterly unperturbed by the look Cole was giving him. Nerissa was about to volunteer to help when a low moaning sound reached her ears, so faint it was barely audible. Goosebumps crept down her flesh for the second time that morning.

"I can see why the locals claim the cave is haunted," Raysel commented.

"It sounded like such a silly rumor when the sun was shining," Nerissa said. "But in this eerie atmosphere, anything seems possible."

Raysel reached up and patted her shoulder in response. She knew the gesture was supposed to be reassuring, but there was a tightness around his eyes that told Nerissa even this simple movement had caused him pain. *That* wasn't the slightest bit reassuring.

"Do you think it will be foggy once we get inside the cave?" Nerissa asked.

Raysel's brow furrowed. "I've never seen fog in the cave leading out of Darnal, but I don't know if every cave is the same. Maybe Alden would know." The furrows in his brow grew deeper as he added, "Speaking of Alden, he should have been here by now."

"Based on the way you described him, he doesn't exactly sound like the punctual type," Rian said.

"You know that type well, don't you?" Cole taunted.

Rian lifted his chin, and he stared down his nose at the sullen twin. He twitched his arm ever so slightly, and Cole jumped back a step, apologizing.

Nerissa smirked, not at Cole's reaction but at Rian's. Though he might not like being reminded of it, Rian really *was* Einar's other delinquent student. At one time, she wouldn't have liked being paired with him for any reason. Now, the idea of having more in common with him brought a pleasant warmth to her chest.

Rian's eyes met hers in a fleeting flicker of a glance before he turned his attention to Raysel. "Am I the only one wondering why Alden told us to bring so much rope? I hope it doesn't mean we will be doing a lot of climbing in there." He pointed to the mound of coiled ropes on the ground beside him for emphasis.

"It does seem strange," Raysel said, studying the pile. "Since the cave was mined for years, I expect the natural tunnel openings have been widened and flattened to allow for carts to be moved through easily. I can't think of any reason why climbing would be necessary unless we have to go into a side tunnel that wasn't actively mined."

The muted jingling of bells from within the fog signaled Alden's approach. "I guess we're about to find out," Nerissa said.

"Hello? I can hear you, so I know you're here. But I can't see a"—Alden's voice trailed off as he censored himself— "thing in this blasted fog."

"I'll come to you," Rian said. He jogged off in the direction of Alden's voice.

A moment later, Rian and Alden emerged from the fog. Just as Alden's hair was adorned with bells, so was the harness of Alden's black and white pinto. More bells decorated the braided sections of the horse's mane. Nerissa couldn't imagine anyone would ever question who this horse belonged to.

Alden dismounted with a flourish of his cloak, and a furry

black head popped out of the open top of one saddlebag. Kuma's tiny nose pointed up, and he sniffed the air curiously. Apparently satisfied with his findings, he gazed down at the group with a doggy grin.

"You brought Kuma with you?" Nerissa blurted out. That was not the first question she had intended to ask Alden, but Kuma's presence was so surprising that the words flew past her lips without thinking.

"That's a strange way to say good morning," Alden replied. "Of course I brought him." The straightforward way he answered made it sound like toting a dog in one's saddlebag was the most natural thing in the world. Kuma snorted softly, and Alden reached up to tousle the fur between his ears.

"I'm sorry, how rude of me. Good morning, Alden," Nerissa said, bowing slightly in apology. She could feel heat rising to her cheeks from embarrassment. *A few months of pretending to be Caeneus and your manners are already slipping*, she chided herself.

Alden bowed in return. "Good morning to you too, Caeneus. There's no need for you to apologize. Kuma always expects to be the center of attention anyway, so it makes sense to acknowledge him first."

He lifted Kuma from the bag, clipped a long leather leash to the dog's collar, and then handed his horse's reins to Rian. Kuma bounded around the area, pausing to inspect each grouping of supplies and sniffing each person in turn. Alden followed behind him, surveying the supplies as well. "I'm glad to see that you took my advice and brought both torches and glow lamps. Why so many though?"

"We thought it was prudent to bring one for each

person," Raysel said.

Alden's lips pressed into a thin line. "That's one of the things we need to discuss before you go in." He dropped to the ground to sit cross-legged and motioned for the others to join him. Kuma bounced into Alden's lap and nestled into the hollow between his knees, watching patiently as the rest of the group settled themselves.

"Is this related to why you ignored our requests to meet before now?" Raysel asked.

Alden folded his arms across his chest. "I am the Governor of the largest province in Chiyo. I'm a busy man. I realize you are eager to retrieve the book as soon as possible, but this was the first day I had available."

Raysel opened his mouth to speak, but Alden cut him off. "I also realize I could have answered your questions before now, but this information is best conveyed in person. No matter how trustworthy the messenger, sensitive material must always be treated with particular care. I'm sure the Ohanzee can appreciate the wisdom in that practice."

"Yes, we can—especially after recent events," Raysel replied. Nerissa would never forget the fierce anger that had painted Raysel's face when he realized that Brigs had betrayed them to the Senka, but his carefully controlled tone betrayed no evidence of that emotion now. "So what is this sensitive information?"

"Let me begin by explaining how the book came to be hidden in the cave. The short version of the story is that my great-grandfather's house once caught on fire. It is, unfortunately, a common hazard in cities."

Nerissa understood that sentiment well. Fire had always been a serious concern in Chiyo since it could spread rapidly from one building to the next in the densely populated capital city. The risk would be the same in any place where people lived close together.

"Even though the book was stored inside a strongbox with other valuables, the extreme heat from the fire damaged the book itself and caused the crystal to break in half. After the incident, a longtime family friend suggested he secure the book by hiding it inside a chest in the abandoned mine," Alden said.

"That's not exactly a rational reaction," Rian broke in.

Kuma's ears perked up, and a low growl rumbled in his throat as he eyed Rian. Clearly, he didn't condone the interruption. Alden patted him soothingly and carried on with his explanation. "No, it isn't, at least not on the surface. This is the point where the story becomes complicated. In his old age, my great-grandfather struggled with his memory. He often mixed up family members' names and became easily confused. Nonetheless, I spent a great deal of time with him when I was a child. You see, he told the *best* stories. Of those, my favorites were the ones he told me about his friend Barr. Barr was an engineer from Marise who lived in Rhea for several years to help design and build the drawbridges. He claimed Barr was actually over three hundred years old."

"No one can live to be that old," Raysel said. "I can see why people said your great-grandfather was confused."

"I thought so too, until recently," Alden agreed. "But before you dismiss the tale entirely, let me go on. According to him, Barr was an expert on crystals in addition to being an engineer. In particular, he claimed that crystals could be made to remember things."

Nerissa leaned forward eagerly. She distinctly recalled Hania telling her a similar story shortly after she woke up in Darnal. "Alden, was your great-grandfather friends with our Chief, Hania?"

Alden cocked his head in surprise. "As a matter of fact, my father was the first member of our family *not* to be an informant. It was a conflict of interest with his role as governor. Both my grandfather and great-grandfather were Ohanzee informants. Why do you ask?"

"Hania once told me he had a friend from Rhea who claimed crystals could be made to remember things."

"Then it seems I wasn't the only one my great-grandfather shared his stories with," Alden said.

Indeed, you were not, Nerissa thought. According to Hania's retelling, the phenomenon could either occur spontaneously or information could be embedded intentionally using a "lost art." She already knew information could intentionally be stored on crystals. That much was confirmed by the explanation accompanying the machine diagrams included with the first portion of the prophecy. The reaction of the books' crystals to her touch was tangible proof of the phenomenon's existence. The more Alden spoke, the less outrageous his great-grandfather's claims seemed to be and the more intriguing his friend Barr became.

Alden continued on. "One of the tales he told me repeatedly was how Barr suggested they hide the heirloom book inside the cave and set a trap to ensure that no one other than the true owner would ever be able to take it."

"Wait," Raysel said. "What exactly did he mean by the 'true owner'? Why would he think that person was anyone other than your great-grandfather?"

That term had piqued Nerissa's interest as well. It gave the impression that Barr knew decades ago about the 'One' the books of prophecy were intended for—but that didn't make sense.

"I asked him the very same question. In response, he gave me the shard I showed you when we met, and he explained that Barr told him someone would eventually come and make the crystal glow. He wouldn't say what made the book so important, but our family was supposed to keep it safe until the true owner came." Alden gave Nerissa a knowing look as he spoke. "And here you are. You should know, he told me many, many fantastical stories. I believed every one of them to be the absolute truth at the time. When I related them back to my father, he dismissed them all as the products of a confused memory and mischievous mind. As I grew up, I also came to realize that much of what he told me was indeed nothing more than tall tales. I believed that right up until I saw that crystal glow in your hand, Caeneus. Even though I stopped believing, I still kept that shard because it reminded me of him. I'm glad that I did. Now I have to wonder how much truth they held. It is possible he and Barr really did set a trap to protect the book, so I think it would be safest if Caeneus went into the cave alone—"

"There's no way we will let the Heir of Chiyo walk into a potential trap with no backup and no protection," Raysel declared without allowing Alden to finish.

Alden's placid expression remained unchanged in spite of Raysel's exclamation. "That's why I told you to bring so much rope—it can serve as his backup," he explained patiently. "The chamber opening is just beyond the fourteenth support pillar, and there are no forks or sharp turns in the tunnel. Caeneus can go in carrying one end of the rope with him. If he runs into trouble, all he has to do is pull on it to signal for help, and it will lead you right to him."

"I *absolutely* will not let Caeneus go in alone," Rian insisted. His blue eyes locked onto Nerissa's as he spoke, and the intensity she saw there made her breath catch in her throat.

Alden shrugged, spreading his upturned hands wide as he did so. "You are, of course, free to do as you wish. I have done my duty by warning you. If there is a trap and you all trigger it, my conscience is clean."

Nerissa realized she was clenching her fists so tightly her nails were digging into her palms. It was vexing that Alden had waited until the last minute to share such critical information. A great deal of deliberation and discussion was required to figure out how to best approach this situation. "Maybe we should go back to the city for today so we can give this more consideration."

Rian drummed his fingers on one knee in irritation. "The last thing I want is for you to be in danger, but no matter how much we talk about it, our options aren't going to change."

To Nerissa's surprise, Raysel nodded in agreement with Rian. "I don't like to make decisions rashly, but I also don't see any benefit in hesitating. There's no question that Caeneus has to go in to retrieve the book, and letting him go in alone isn't an option we can accept. I am Caeneus' guardian, and I've already sworn to protect him—with my life, if necessary. The two of us will take the rope and go in together. The rest of you

25

will wait here and come if we signal for help."

"I second the idea of sending in as few people as possible," Rian said. "And it makes sense for you to be the one to go—except for one detail you're glossing over." He reached over and patted Raysel's arm, causing his friend to let out an involuntary grunt of pain. "If Caeneus is going to be in danger, he needs the guardian at his side to be in top form. Right now, that person isn't you."

Nerissa watched as the two went back and forth, growing progressively more annoyed that they were talking about her as if she weren't there. This was not a decision that was solely up to them, and yet neither of them bothered to ask for her opinion.

Raysel scowled and clamped his hand over his injured arm. "I am perfectly capable of wielding my sword left-handed."

"You are better with a sword left-handed than many of the Ohanzee are with their dominant hand, but you aren't better than me," Rian argued. "In this situation, I am better able to protect Caeneus than you."

Raysel's expression darkened as he struggled to think of a counter to Rian's argument, and Nerissa took the opportunity to interject. "I will go in with Rian," she declared. When Raysel opened his mouth to argue, she cut him off. "Consider that to be a command from the Heir."

3

A BROKEN GLOW LAMP

Nerissa

No matter how many uncertainties Nerissa had about going into the cave, she knew the security of the knots holding the rope segments of the lifeline together was one thing she wouldn't have to worry about. Raysel tied each one of those himself, and he had poured every ounce of his frustration into the task. If the knots could survive his wrath, it was unlikely that anything in the cave could pull them apart.

"I think we are as ready as we can be," Nerissa said as she reached out to take the end of the rope from Raysel. As the tips of her fingers brushed the coarse fibers, he jerked his hand away.

"It's not too late to change your mind," he said.

The imploring look on Raysel's face was such a rare sight that Nerissa was almost tempted to reconsider her decision to go into the cave with Rian. She *might* have been tempted, had she not noticed that he offered the rope to her with his left hand rather than his right. Regardless of how strong he was, he had ten stitches in his arm. Going with Rian ensured that Raysel wouldn't worsen his injury by pushing himself too hard on her behalf. More importantly, if she were to be injured, it spared him from blaming himself for not doing more to protect her.

Raysel took her hesitation as an opportunity to press his argument further. "I am not only your personal guardian; I am also First Swordsman of the Ohanzee. Even with my right arm injured, you know I am still completely capable of protecting you."

"I know that," Nerissa said, feeling her resolve weakening.

It was then that Rian strode over to the pair and unceremoniously plucked the rope from Raysel's hand. "The First Swordsman of the Ohanzee should know better than to argue with a direct command from the Heir," Rian admonished. He gave the end of the rope to Nerissa and then slung the pack containing the two torches and the flint-and-steel fire striker onto his back.

Raysel huffed with frustration, but he didn't pursue the issue any further. Instead, his eyes locked with Nerissa's. "I'm sure the trap Alden spoke of has to be related to the warning in the prophecy. If anything happens—anything—pull this three times, and I will come as fast as I can."

"I know." Nerissa squeezed Raysel's hand reassuringly. "We'll be careful."

Rian clapped Raysel on the shoulder—his good shoulder this time. "I'll protect Caeneus the same way you would. With my life, if necessary."

"Hold it," Nerissa broke in. She pointed her pinky finger at Raysel, shaking it in the air in front of him as she spoke. "*You* should know better than to talk like that. We made a promise."

A hint of pink rose in Raysel's cheeks, and he would have looked genuinely abashed if there hadn't been a spark of amusement in his green eyes. "I haven't forgotten it."

Seemingly satisfied with his answer, Nerissa rounded on Rian. "The whole reason why I began training was to learn to protect myself so that no one will ever need to sacrifice their health for my safety. My life is no more valuable than anyone else's. So, while I am grateful for your willingness to fight by my side for the sake of Chiyo, I do not want anyone swearing to die for me. You may recite that nonsense in your head if you must. But if I hear those words uttered once more, I will not hesitate to issue an edict banning the use of that phrase."

Rian folded his arms across his chest, a lopsided smile on his lips. "I'd be a hypocrite to argue with you after lecturing Raysel for doing the same thing a few minutes ago, wouldn't I?" he asked. He inclined his head toward the cave entrance. "Shall we go?"

Although Rian's answer was agreeable enough, Nerissa couldn't squelch the feeling that she had lost the argument. "Yes, let's go," she replied. She picked up her glow lamp and followed Rian.

No sooner did she reached the mouth of the cave than there came a sharp tug from the other end of the rope. She looked back, intending to give Raysel one final, confident smile and found that he and the others had already turned into formless shadows within the thick mist. Instead, she patted her chest where the fire-fire crystal pendant hung and gave the rope a gentle tug in return before stepping inside.

———————————◆———————————

In the absolute blackness of the cave, Nerissa's and Rian's glow lamps appeared to be little more than floating white orbs that bobbed in synchrony with the soft tapping of their owners' footsteps. The darkness was so complete that it appeared to encroach on the soft glow rather than be scattered by it. However, once Nerissa's eyes had adjusted, the lamps were more than enough to illuminate the surrounding tunnel.

She walked beside Rian in silence, her ears straining to detect any peculiar sounds. There were few noises to be heard, aside from their footsteps and the scrape of the rope as it dragged along the cave floor. There was no sign of the spirit or Alden's trap so far and not even a hint of the howling that fueled the locals' claims that the mine was haunted. Still, she flinched at every unexplained creak and occasional crunch of pebbles underfoot. It was one thing to bravely state that she wouldn't let the warning prevent her from fetching the book. It was another thing entirely to march into the unknown on wobbly knees.

Suddenly, a low mumbling whisper reached her ears. Nerissa froze as the hairs on the back of her neck stood on end. The voice had seemed so close that it could have come from right beside her. The glow lamp tumbled from her grasp, forgotten in her haste to reach for Harbinger's hilt. The tinkle of broken glass echoed off the tunnel walls as it hit the floor.

Rian, who had continued walking unaware of her alarm, whirled around at the clatter. By the time he turned to face her, he had already drawn Bane. The light from the remaining glow lamp caught on the blade, flashing up and down the length of the bare metal as the lantern swung in Rian's free hand. "What's wrong?"

"I thought I heard a voice," Nerissa said, glancing around nervously.

Rian's shoulders sagged, and he returned Bane to its sheath. "Of course you did. I was talking to you."

Nerissa's cheeks flushed with shame as she stared down at the shattered remains of her lamp. "That was *you*? Why were you whispering?"

Rian deliberately avoided meeting her eyes. "It's really quiet in here. I didn't want to speak too loudly and startle you, but it seems I did anyway."

"It's my fault for overreacting," Nerissa said, rubbing her forehead while internally scolding herself for her foolishness. "I need to get my nerves under control before it causes more problems."

"One broken lamp isn't a big problem," Rian said. "We still have mine. Do you want to light one of the torches?"

Nerissa shook her head. "No, we don't know how long they will last, and it's best to save them until we absolutely need them. I can see well enough as long as you lead the way."

Rian nodded. "Make sure you stay close to me," he said.

"What did you say before?" Nerissa asked after they had walked in silence for a few minutes.

She heard Rian inhale, and then his answer came in a rush of words as if he were reluctant to repeat them. "I said I felt

31

bad about being so hard on Raysel earlier."

"I don't think you were being unreasonable," Nerissa said.

"I insisted on being the one to come with you as much for his own good as for yours. He doesn't ever talk about it, but I know he feels guilty for not being able to protect the Heiress on the night of the attack." Rian hesitated before adding, "He's too stubborn to admit when he needs help, and I don't want him to end up feeling guilty if something were to happen to you."

Despite her anxiety, a warm feeling welled up inside her. Their concern for Raysel was another thing they had in common. "That was exactly my reasoning when I said I would go with you."

"I really will protect you with the same vigor as he would," Rian said.

He glanced over his shoulder at her, and his eyes held the same fierce determination that Nerissa had seen before they entered the cave. When Raysel spoke of protecting her then, he had said "we," referring to the Ohanzee as a group. But Rian had said "I." It was a subtle distinction. Maybe she was reading too much into it, but the look in his eyes—both then and now—made her wonder if the difference actually *was* significant. She shook her head to clear her thoughts. She was reading too much into that. Rian wouldn't think of "Caeneus" in that way.

When she didn't reply right away, Rian said, "Are you sure that Raysel is actually adding length to the rope and not just following on the other end?"

A chuckle had escaped Nerissa's lips before she realized

it. "If he were, I'm pretty sure he would have come running when I dropped the lantern."

Rian did laugh at that. "I have no doubt he would have."

They walked in silence again, stopping intermittently to check the numbers on the wooden support pillars. "I'm glad the fog didn't go very far past the entrance," Rian commented.

He's trying to make small talk to help me calm down. Nerissa smiled at the realization, simultaneously feeling pleased by his kindness and disappointed in herself for needing it. "Me too," she said, fumbling to think of something more to add. *You've had years of etiquette training. Why can't you think of a single thing to say?*

The rope suddenly rose from the ground and pulled taut before slipping from her grasp. "Wait! I think we've run out of rope. Either that or it's caught on something." She bent down and gave it a single, firm tug, afraid anything more would be mistaken as a call for help. Despite her efforts, it didn't budge.

Rian walked back to the last support pillar they had passed and held his glow lamp out to better see the surface. The number fourteen had been seared into the wood at eye level. "Alden said the chamber was just past the fourteenth support pillar, so we're not far from the book now. Let's go on ahead, and we can pick up the rope on the way back."

Nerissa hesitated. It seemed unwise to leave behind their sole connection to the others when the book, and whatever protected it, awaited them within the chamber ahead. She looked to Rian, who stood beside the pillar patiently waiting for her response. He had remained calm and collected this whole time, while her own nerves had her jumping at every sound. In this case, it was best to let cooler heads prevail.

She laid the rope down near the pillar so it would be easy to find again when they passed on the way back. "Alright. Let's go."

4

THE SPIRIT IN THE CAVE

Nerissa

The main chamber of the cave was both considerably taller and wider than the tunnel leading up to it. An opening in the far wall, which must once have led deeper into the mine, was now filled with fallen rocks and dirt as a result of the collapse decades before. Debris had spilled out from it, spewing broken stone halfway across the chamber. Rusted pickaxes and buckets lay haphazardly scattered across the floor, untouched since the day they had been hastily discarded by fleeing miners.

Nerissa and Rian moved cautiously, following the wall and pausing every so often to examine the various items they came across. Everything in sight was blanketed in a thick layer of dust. Nerissa peered uncertainly overhead as the rotten wood supports groaned, straining under the weight of the surrounding rock and years of neglect. So far, there was no sign of a trap. If there was a spirit crystal protecting the book, it must be hidden somewhere or covered in detritus like everything else.

"That must be what we're looking for," Rian said, pointing to a large chest against the wall a few feet ahead. "The exterior looks too fancy for a tool or supply chest, and it has a lot less dust on it than anything else in here."

"It does look out of place," Nerissa agreed.

"There's not even a lock," Rian observed once they were standing in front of the trunk. "I'll open it. You should stand back in case opening the lid triggers the trap."

"No," Nerissa said firmly. "*This* is the reason why I came here in the first place. Alden and the prophecy both told us to beware of what is down here. The trap is meant to keep anyone other than the 'true owner' from taking the book. If either one of us opens the chest, it should be me."

She deliberately maintained a placid expression while Rian struggled to find an argument against her logic. He pinched the bridge of his nose, closed his eyes, and exhaled heavily. "Fine," he said flatly.

Nerissa waited until she was kneeling in front of the chest with her back to him before allowing herself to smirk in triumph. She hadn't expected him to give in so quickly.

The latch mechanism gave an audible click as she pressed the release, but the hinge, frozen from years of corrosion, refused to move. She pried at the metal hasp with her fingernails to no avail. Frustrated, she turned to ask Rian for help and found him gazing down at her with an amused smile on his lips. The phrase "to win the battle but not the war" immediately sprang to Nerissa's mind.

Gritting her teeth, she turned back to the trunk without saying a word. She balled her fist and swiftly brought it down against the lid directly above the latch. It popped up a fraction of an inch, barely enough for her to slip her fingers under it. Rian snorted in annoyance at the shrill squeak the hasp emitted as she forced it the rest of the way back.

Nerissa hesitated before pushing the lid open, taking a deep breath and mentally bracing herself for what may be inside—or for what may come out. Finally, she slowly eased it upward, the hinges rasping in rusty protest with every inch of movement. Rian hovered so closely behind her that she couldn't tell whether it was trepidation that made her skin tingle or the feeling of his breath on the back of her neck. Was he trying to hold the glow lamp closer or to shield her from whatever danger lay within? Either way, she felt grateful.

But once the lid was fully open, nothing unusual happened. Another, smaller container was nested inside. The smaller box was utterly utilitarian in design and made entirely of metal. Its only distinguishing features were the handles on each side and a crust of soot that covered most of the surface. This had to be the fire-damaged strongbox belonging to Alden's great-grandfather.

There was no way to open it without removing it first. Nerissa grasped the handles and attempted to lift it from the chest, but it was too heavy.

In the middle of her third attempt, Rian cleared his throat. "I don't think you're going to be able to carry that yourself. I know you're concerned about the warning, but the reason why *I* came in here is to help you."

Nerissa chewed her bottom lip thoughtfully. Years of archery training with Einar had made her upper body strong, while conditioning with the Ohanzee had made her even stronger, and yet she couldn't lift as much as many men. Some things just weren't physically possible. Still, if she wanted to maintain her disguise, she couldn't call attention to that fact. And then an idea occurred to her.

"It's probably also too heavy for you to pick up, and doing so might trigger the trap. Let's each take one side. If the trap works like the other crystals, it'll probably be alright as long as I'm touching the box as well," she said.

"That's reasonable," Rian replied. He hung the glow lamp around his wrist and waited for Nerissa to grip a handle before picking up the other one himself. The wooden supports overhead creaked again, louder this time, and a mass of pebbles clattered to the floor nearby as they removed the box from the chest.

"This one doesn't have a lock on it eith—," Rian started to say, but he never got the chance to finish his sentence.

The handle of the strongbox was ripped from Nerissa's grasp as it and Rian flew across the chamber. The box hit the far wall with enough force to gouge a crater. Books and papers rained out of it onto the ground below. Rian's body struck the wall a split second later, and the lamp on his arm shattered, its light winking out as glowing glass fragments sprayed over his sprawled form like a shower of falling stars.

"Rian!" Nerissa screamed his name so loudly her throat burned, but her voice was drowned out as the pitch-black chamber swelled with a cacophony of sound.

Hundreds of voices, too many to distinguish, cried out from every direction, seemingly emitted from within the surrounding stone. Incoherent sobbing. A child begging to see his father. A woman's forlorn wails. A chorus joined together singing the mournful notes of a funeral dirge. One voice—a man's—stood out above them all repeating, "The book must remain safe."

Tears sprang to Nerissa's eyes as a crippling sadness washed over her. The sensation was so intense that it almost sent her to her knees. The sorrow she felt over losing her parents came flooding back, making her feel like she was reliving those first miserable days after awakening in Darnal. As the voices climbed to a crescendo, wisps of bluish light seeped from the crystalline deposits in the walls like tendrils of fog. They swirled together in the center of the chamber, gradually growing more distinct until they formed a luminous, human-like silhouette. It flared in and out of existence like rhythmic lightning. The apparition in front of her was neither the lingering ghost of a deceased miner nor a wandering soul unaware of its own death, Nerissa realized. This spirit was an amalgamation of the anguish and grief felt by the villagers at the loss of their beloveds.

If this creature was the result of triggering the trap Barr had set to protect the book, it was a formidable trap, indeed. For the first time in her life, Nerissa was horrified of the power that could be harnessed by crystals.

There was no time for her to wonder how such a thing was possible, however. Each time the spirit flared into being, she could see that it had drawn another step closer to Rian's limp body. Its strobing light transformed Nerissa's vision into little more than a series of images haltingly stitched together.

Flash.

The spirit towered over Rian, drawing one arm back in preparation to strike.

39

Flash.

It brought its arm down, slashing across Rian's back and ripping open the pack he wore. His agonized howl briefly rose above the other sounds before being swallowed by the woeful voices.

Nerissa's heart was rent in two by the sound of his suffering, yet with it came relief at knowing he was alive. Fear, sharper than the memory of her grief, pierced Nerissa's gut like an ice-cold lance, sending chills radiating from the soles of her feet to the tips of her fingers.

"Stop!" she shrieked as the spirit recoiled to hit Rian again.

And, surprisingly, it did.

In the blink of an eye, the spirit was looming over her, arm still drawn back and poised to strike. Nerissa dropped to the ground and rolled in an attempt to dodge the anticipated blow, bracing herself for the pain that was sure to come. Instead, as its arm came down, a tingling wave passed harmlessly through her.

The spirit froze in place, and a woman's voice suddenly carried above the clamor. "That person, the One who is no more, the One who has become another…," the voice began, reciting the description of Nerissa from the prophecy.

Then the spirit disappeared and reappeared near Rian. The man's voice from earlier boomed out over the woman's saying, "The book must remain safe," so loudly that a shower of stones shook loose from the ceiling. Rian bellowed as the spirit battered him yet again.

Heedless of the danger to herself, Nerissa stumbled

across the chamber to put herself between Rian and the spirit. "Stop!" she commanded.

But this time, the spirit did not obey. In the glow of its light, Nerissa could see that Rian's arm was draped over a thick, leather-bound book. A crystal glinted from the spine. He's lying on the book! She felt the same strange tingling as the spirit's arm passed through her, and Rian yelled as it thrashed him a third time. The spirit may not be able to hurt her, but she couldn't keep it from hurting Rian either.

"The book must remain safe," came the man's voice, almost as if it were egging the spirit on.

Nerissa's mind raced. If the spirit was supposed to keep the book safe, perhaps it would be an effective shield. She dropped to the ground and yanked the object from beneath Rian's arm. Clutching it to her chest, she rolled on her side until her back was pressed against Rian.

But her efforts were unnecessary. The instant she took the book into her arms, the spirit froze and began to dissipate. The constant barrage of voices slowly faded until solely the woman's voice remained, tremulous yet unfaltering. "...the One who is no more, the One who has become another, the One who was seen before, the Reflection, will appear from the shadows." The spirit bowed deeply as the last word resonated through the chamber and then winked out of existence.

Stunned, Nerissa stared into total darkness trying to comprehend what just happened and to determine what she needed to do next. All she could see was the blue afterimage of the spirit that had burned into her eyes. She hugged the book tightly as if it were a ward to prevent the spirit's return. Perhaps it was. She didn't intend to stay long enough to find out.

Still clinging to the book with one hand, she crawled toward where she had last seen the torches. She hardly noticed when something sharp—probably a shard of glass from the broken glow lamp—pierced through the fabric of her pants and cut the skin on her knee. Undaunted, she persisted onward, scrabbling blindly until she touched something familiar—the base of one of the torches.

"Found one!" she declared to no one in particular, but her victory was short-lived. She ran her hand up its length searching for the end covered with waxed cloth only to discover that the torch had been severed cleanly in half. With a curse, she flung it as far as she could and frantically continued searching for the other torch, hoping it was intact.

Finally, as her pounding heartbeat counted every passing second, her palm brushed the handle of the torch. Nerissa grabbed it and cheered in relief when she determined it was in one piece. After shoving the end of it into the waistband of her pants, she hastily crawled back to Rian.

The flint-and-steel fire striker had been in the pocket of the backpack. All she could do was hope that it had been spared from the spirit's fury. If the small tin box containing the fire striker had been scattered among the rest of the debris, her chances of finding it now was slim.

As Nerissa gingerly patted the torn remains of the pack on Rian's back, her fingers dragged across something sticky and warm on the canvas. Inhaling sharply, she set her jaw and redoubled her effort to find the tin. The metallic scent filling her nose told her what the liquid was, and the knowledge further fueled her desire to escape as quickly as possible. "Can you hear me, Rian?" she asked.

He babbled something unintelligible in response, but that was enough to answer her question.

"I'm going to get us out of here and back to the rope as fast as I can," she said, as much for her own benefit as for his. Her heart leaped with joy when her fingers finally stumbled across the button to the front pocket.

"Can't...see...," Rian moaned as she withdrew the tin box. She emptied the contents into her hand, and a cloth came out along with the flint and steel. Unsure what the cloth was for, she hastily cast it aside.

"Don't worry. I can't see anything either," Nerissa answered as she rocked back and pulled the torch from her waistband. "I'm trying to fix that now."

Rian grunted, but he didn't say anything more.

She put the torch on the floor in front of her, wedging the book between her knees so both of her hands would be free. The flint piece nearly slipped from her trembling fingers, but somehow she held onto it. Although she had watched others start campfires numerous times, Nerissa had never done it herself. The task looked simple enough at the time. All she had to do to produce sparks was strike the steel piece downward against the flint.

Holding the pieces over the waxed end of the torch, she swiftly brought the steel down to the flint. Or, at least, she tried. Her hands were shaking so much the first time that she completely missed, swiping fruitlessly through the air.

On the next try, the steel struck home, throwing out sparks in a shimmering spray. They fell downward and

43

disappeared without producing so much as a brief glow on the cloth. Nerissa repeated the process over and over, pounding the flint with a futile flurry of ineffective strikes.

"I need flames," she chanted under her breath. Her lungs burned from the effort, and her throat was clenched tight with frustration and fear. Panting, she dropped her arms to her side, struggling to catch her breath. Every one of her thoughts was focused with razor sharpness on a single goal.

Fire.

A sudden heat flared between her breasts, so intense it almost felt like her skin had been seared. At the same time, the scent of burning cloth filled her nose as flames roared out from the head of the torch.

Nerissa gasped in surprise and prodded at the warm spot on her chest, but there was no pain, and she had more pressing concerns to deal with. She nudged Rian, wincing sympathetically at the sight of his back where long hair and blood intermixed in a black and scarlet mass. "Time to leave," she said. "I'm going to help you stand up."

"Moving hurts too much," Rian groaned.

Nerissa wedged herself beside him and wrapped his arm around her shoulder despite his protests. As she attempted to help him to his feet, his shirt began to ride up, and Rian struggled to cling to its hem. "This would be easier if you held onto *me* instead of your shirt," Nerissa said, but he didn't loosen his grip.

Once she managed to get him into a sitting position, he slumped forward with his elbows on his knees. "Just leave me here and come back with the others."

Nerissa stood, careful to maintain a tight grip on the book. Though he spoke softly, Rian's words echoed through the chamber. She remembered his insistence that he would not allow her to come here alone. An indescribable mixture of dread and resolve rose up from the pit of her stomach and rooted her feet firmly to the ground. There was no way she would leave him behind, not even temporarily.

"If you can't walk, then we'll have to do this the hard way," Nerissa said, silently thanking Raysel for teaching her a basic carrying technique as part of her training. She bent on one knee beside Rian and carefully nestled the book in the space between her leg and waist. Ignoring his protests, she draped one of his arms around her neck. Ducking down to wrap her elbow behind his knee, she lifted him from his feet so that his torso was fully supported across her shoulders.

"You can't carry me out of here," Rian said.

Nerissa huffed under the pressure of his additional weight. "What I *can't* do is carry all of this and you at the same time. I need you to hold onto the torch for me. Can you manage that?"

"I can do anything I have to," Rian asserted despite the fact that his voice wavered with pain.

"Likewise," Nerissa replied, passing the torch behind her so he could take it with his free hand. She moved the book to hold it at her hip next to Harbinger and away from Rian. The last thing they needed was for it to brush up against him and accidentally resummon the creature.

Using the wall to stabilize herself, she pushed up to a standing position and then began to stagger slowly across the chamber. Her thighs strained. Her unsteady knees threatened to buckle with every step, but she kept moving.

"I knew you were strong, but I didn't know you were this strong," Rian said. "You're full of surprises. That's one of the things I like about you." He rambled on, but his voice was so weak and her own breathing so labored that she couldn't make out anything else until he said, "I'm sorry I lied to you."

"Lied...to me?" Nerissa panted in an attempt to keep him talking. His initial comments didn't pass unnoticed, but there was no point in taking them to heart when Rian was obviously delirious. Still, it didn't matter what he said. As long as she could hear his voice, she would know he was conscious.

"Raysel really means it when he says he would die to protect you. I can't go quite that far. I can't die until I stop my father."

"Well, worry not...you won't be dying today," she managed to say. She supposed she should be grateful to have one less person willing to throw themselves on a sword for her sake, regardless of the reasoning. After all, that was what she said she wanted.

Rian made a noise that vaguely sounded like a laugh and said nothing more. Nerissa willed herself to put one foot in front of the other, afraid that if she paused to rest she wouldn't be able to make her legs move again. She persisted onward, going through the opening that led to the tunnel and back to pillar fourteen. Kneeling briefly, she let Rian slide to the floor and then picked up the rope, tugging it as hard as she could. She was supposed to pull three times to call for help, but she kept pulling until three floating white orbs bobbed into sight. Only then did she give in to her exhaustion and slump down beside Rian on the stone floor.

5

COINCIDENCES

Nerissa

The hallway door had barely closed behind Raysel before Nerissa flung off her blankets. She was feeling far too restless to lie in bed waiting for his return. Ever since the encounter with the spirit in the cave, the hours had passed by in a whirlwind of activity, and Nerissa's racing pulse had just recently begun to taper. Leaning over the edge, she dragged out her pack and slipped her hand into one of the small interior pockets. She pulled the sparkling perfume bottle from Raysel out of its velvet pouch and unscrewed the top, inhaling deeply. The sweet aroma of roses blended with strawberries overwhelmed her senses, loosening her shoulders and settling her swirling thoughts.

After savoring one final sniff, she returned the bottle to its place inside the pack and hopped out of bed. Her feet sank into the plush carpet, and she dug her toes into the pile, relishing the blissful softness. This was one of the most upscale inns in Rhea, chosen because it suited a group of merchants invited to do business directly with the governor himself. The

47

carpet was such a subtle luxury that she might not have noticed it a year ago, yet it stood out to her now. The sensation almost offset the soreness that stiffened her lower back and thighs as she paced. Almost.

With Rian now recovering under the watchful eyes of the hospital staff a few blocks away, the rest of the group had returned to the inn. Nerissa herself had narrowly dodged being subjected to an examination as well. *That* would have been awkward, to say the least. It had been avoided only by her repeated insistence that the blood on her clothing was the result of carrying Rian and not personal injury. Worried that admission of even the slightest wound would result in a full exam, she had waited until they were back at the inn to mention the cut on her knee. Raysel had practically coated her in antiseptic and bandages, barely giving her the opportunity to sponge off the grime and change clothes before bundling her into bed. Although he dressed her knee with the utmost care, he had bombarded her all the while with a storm of questions about what happened inside the cave. Answering him had been nearly as exhausting as the experience itself.

Nerissa paused in front of the standing mirror and lifted the bottom of her tunic and undershirt. Hanging at the base of her sternum, as always, was the fire-fire crystal pendant. Behind it—in the exact size and shape of the crystal—was a blackened scorch mark where the gauze had been reduced to a sooty char. She had first noticed the burn while changing, but based on Raysel's reaction to the small cut on her knee, she had decided to wait until she got a better look at it before mentioning it. Studying the reflected mark now, all doubts about its origin were driven from her mind.

The pendant swung innocuously against her chest as she

pulled her shirts back down and proceeded to the table where the newest book lay. Her fingers brushed the leather cover, which was mottled with brown and black patches from the fire long ago. The intricate filigree decorating the front was still visible, though little more than a trace of the original gold leaf remained. It surrounded a central design that consisted of four triangles arranged along the edges of a square to form the shape of a diamond. The more Nerissa studied it, the more familiar the design seemed, but she couldn't quite place why.

Despite everything that happened in the cave, the crystal shard had miraculously remained tucked into the book's spine. As Nerissa pried it out, the soft glow it emitted highlighted the network of fractures riddling the stone. Having already seen its other half, she was not surprised to see the extent of the heat damage. In fact, considering the sheer number of cracks present, it was amazing the stone hadn't shattered entirely.

Nerissa's hand trembled as the thought of shattering crystals reminded her of those that had broken in the days leading up to the masquerade. There was a superstition that said shattering crystals were supposed to be an omen of significant change, and yet she had been too preoccupied to pay much attention to the occurrence. If she had taken heed of the warning, would the outcome of Casimer's attack have been different?

In a deliberate effort to distract herself from that unproductive line of thought, she placed the shard on the table and opened the book. She reached for the upper corner of the inner cover, no longer caring that she had promised to wait until Raysel returned to read the next section of the prophecy.

As she did so, the knob to the hall door clicked, and Nerissa swatted the book closed. With a guilty flush staining her cheeks, she whirled around in time to see Raysel step inside while balancing a tray of food in one hand. He glanced suspiciously between her face and the book on the table, but he looked amused rather than annoyed.

"Don't tell me you thought I actually *believed* you would stay in bed once I left the room," Raysel teased.

A fleeting smile crossed Nerissa's lips in response. As much as she wanted to eat right away, there wouldn't be much time to talk before Desta and the others came back from the dining room. "I need to tell you something while we're alone."

"What is it?" Raysel asked. His amused suspicion turned genuine upon hearing her odd tone of voice. He set the tray on the table beside the book, and tendrils of steam curled appetizingly above the two bowls of beef with barley.

"I know I said earlier that my only injury was the cut on my knee—" Nerissa began.

"Where else were you hurt?" Raysel interrupted.

Nerissa shook her head and rushed on. "I wasn't hurt. It'll be easier to explain if I show you," she said, and then she pulled up her shirts for the second time. Upon seeing the bare skin of her stomach, Raysel quickly averted his gaze.

"You can look—I have my wraps on," Nerissa said. "That's what you need to see. I haven't taken off the ones I wore in the cave yet. I was waiting until I showed you this to change them."

Raysel slowly raised his eyes from the floor, still hesitant to look regardless of her reassurances.

"How did that happen?" Raysel asked, perplexed. "There was no burn mark on the outside of your clothes. I would have seen it."

"So you're shy now, but you weren't afraid to look closely before?" Nerissa pointed out with a smirk.

Raysel's lips twisted as he realized she was teasing him. "That was the outside of your clothes," he said, the tips of his ears turning red.

"You were looking out for my well-being then, and the situation is no different now," Nerissa said. The wraps she wore around her chest and torso were more than sufficient to alleviate any concerns about compromising her modesty. "I think the gauze must have gotten burned in the process of lighting the torch after the attack. I was so nervous that I couldn't get it to catch." She explained her desperation and difficulties with the flint and steel, the heat she felt flare up just before the torch lit, and how the flames seemed to spring up on their own.

Raysel grasped her wrist. "Wait. Are you telling me that you were trying to use the flint and steel without a char cloth?"

"Char cloth?"

Raysel's brows rose. "You're supposed to use the sparks from the flint to light the char cloth first and then use *that* to start the fire."

Nerissa's eyes widened. Now that Raysel mentioned it, she did remember seeing him holding something else whenever he used the flint and steel. "So that's what the cloth was for!"

"You really didn't use the char cloth?"

"No. It was in the container with the flint and steel, but I didn't know what it was for."

Raysel rubbed his chin in consideration. "No wonder you had such a hard time starting the fire. It's extremely difficult to do without the char cloth. I suppose one of those sparks *could* have landed on the torch head and smoldered, but I doubt it."

He reached out and lifted the leather cord from around her neck, cupping the pendant in his hand to examine it more closely. The stone itself was unmarked, but the delicate goldwork surrounding it was laced with soot. "It feels warm to the touch but no more so than any other object would be after being in close contact with someone's body." Turning his attention to the blackened mark on the gauze, he asked, "Did it burn your skin too?"

"No, there's not even a red mark," Nerissa assured him. "It certainly felt hot enough to burn me at the time, but despite that, it didn't harm me in the slightest. It's too far-fetched to think the mark wasn't caused by the pendant. The timing between when I felt the heat and when the flames appeared is too coincidental. It's almost as if thinking about fire *made* it produce the flames."

"I don't know," Raysel said incredulously. "I've read dozens of books on the uses of crystals, and none of them ever mentioned being able to make one do something. We know crystals have many uses—your voice-changing necklace and Ildiko's healing stones are merely two examples. But they always function passively. You wear the necklace, and the stones alter the sound of your voice whether you are aware of it or not."

"I've never heard of it happening either," she said. Her eyes locked with his, and she added, "Still, as strange as it was, I can't deny what I experienced."

Raysel held her gaze for a moment before nodding in agreement. "Can you make it happen again?"

Nerissa took the necklace from him and stared into the crimson stone while trying to summon up the same urgency she felt before. Her eyes narrowed to slits as she concentrated, but it was of no use. Nothing happened—not a glint, not a glimmer, and definitely not any heat. Sighing, she handed the pendant back to Raysel.

"Let me try," he said. He closed his eyes, and his brow furrowed in concentration. "I'm focusing on fire as hard as I can, but I don't feel the stone getting any warmer."

"I don't see anything happening either," Nerissa said.

Raysel opened his eyes and frowned. "I don't think you should wear this until we figure out exactly how it burned the gauze."

Nerissa snatched the pendant from his hand and clutched it tightly in her fist. "I've worn this every day for months, and nothing has happened until now. Maybe there was something in the cave that caused it to behave oddly," she suggested.

"No. You noticed something strange about the crystal before," Raysel countered. "I remember you thought it glowed the day I gave it back to you. We assumed it was a trick of the light at the time, but maybe it wasn't."

Nerissa bit her bottom lip. She couldn't argue with that. The crystal *had* felt oddly warm while she watched the others help put out the fire in Darci's workshop. She hadn't given it any further consideration since then, but perhaps it actually had been significant.

"This crystal is the first thing that belonged to me since

Casimer's attack, and it's also a precious gift from you. Even if I'm just being overly sentimental, I'm not going to part with it easily," Nerissa said. "Besides, we have a better chance of learning more about it if I keep it close."

Raysel gave her a reluctant smile. He didn't like it, but she did have a point. "If you feel that strongly about it, I won't press the issue. Promise me that you will be careful with it, and you'll let me know right away if you notice anything out of the ordinary."

"I promise," Nerissa swore. She extended her pinky finger to him, and he hooked it with his to shake on their agreement.

"Should we eat now or check the book?" Raysel asked.

"That's a silly question," Nerissa said. Her hands were already stroking the book's cover. "Books always come before food—unless you can eat and read at the same time, of course. This one is far too old to do that with, however."

Raysel cast one longing look at the steaming bowls. "The soup can wait."

The binding crackled, and bits of leather flaked off onto the table as Nerissa opened the cover. She peeled away the fabric to reveal the next section of the prophecy and another diagram.

> The fourth section of the prophecy is as follows:
> Deep in the caves, the inborn talent of the Reflection will draw a spark from the Heart of Fire that will ultimately return an ancient power to the world.
> They will journey through the ruins in the

mountains to the place where time stands still. Here, the lost suspension technique is still remembered. The Reflection will confront the Destroyer using this technique in order to retake the throne without staining their own hands with blood.

Nerissa and Raysel finished reading at almost the exact same time.

"It couldn't be describing…," Raysel began.

"It has to be! There's no other logical explanation. This *must* be the Heart of Fire!" Nerissa exclaimed as she fumbled to pull the pendant out from under her shirt again.

Raysel grabbed her hand. "Let's not be hasty."

Nerissa's jaw dropped. "Hasty?" she squeaked. "It says I have an inborn talent that will draw a spark from the Heart of Fire. We were *just* debating how I could have used the crystal to light the torch. This 'ancient power' has to be the explanation."

"I'll admit that I'm intrigued, but the prophecy doesn't tell us much. Is this ancient power a good thing?"

Nerissa's mouth opened and closed as she tried to formulate a counter argument. "You're right, it doesn't tell us much," she relented. "How could it be a bad thing if it can be used to stop Casimer?"

"It doesn't say the power can be used to stop Casimer. It says Casimer's actions can be suspended. Suspending an action isn't the same as stopping it."

"Aren't you getting hung up on one little word?" Nerissa pointed to the second paragraph. "It says right here that the lost technique can be used to remove Casimer from power without bloodshed."

"I realize taking back Chiyo without bloodshed is the outcome you want most. Yet something about the prophecy's wording makes me doubt the solution is as straightforward as it seems."

Nerissa thrummed her fingers on the page. Raysel did have a point, though she hated to admit it. She had only seen what she wanted to see in the prophecy's words, but that wasn't necessarily the correct interpretation.

A knock came from the hallway door, and Desta popped her head in before either of them could answer. She looked past the pair, eyeing the untouched tray of food on the table.

"I came up to take the tray back to the kitchen for you, but you haven't even eaten yet!" she proclaimed after stepping inside.

Nerissa pressed the fabric lining back into place and closed the book's cover. "We can talk more about this later," she said. She took one of the bowls and sat down at the table with Raysel.

Desta studied the book's cover, tracing her index finger around each of the four triangles in the center of the design. "Is this the book you brought back from the cave?"

"Yes," Nerissa said between bites.

Desta's head tilted to the side thoughtfully, but she didn't say anything more.

"Why don't you have a seat?" Raysel invited.

"Oh, no. I'll leave the two of you alone. I was planning to

do some writing," Desta said, turning away so quickly it made Nerissa wonder what the girl was hiding.

She broke off a piece of bread and dunked it into her soup, watching as Desta pulled a notebook and pen out from under her pillow. In recent days, it had become apparent to both Nerissa and Raysel that Desta's behavior had changed. Instead of spending her free time socializing with the twins, she had been withdrawn and pensive. Nerissa had assumed Desta was still angry with the twins for peeping on her, but she'd been smiling and laughing with them at breakfast the last two mornings. Since it seemed they had been forgiven, there had to be another cause. She strongly suspected it had something to do with whatever Desta was writing in her notebook. The first thing Desta had done after checking into the inn was seek out a stationary store, and she had subsequently spent at least an hour each day scribbling onto the journal's pages.

Nerissa glanced across the table at Raysel to find that he was also eyeing Desta curiously. He cleared his throat casually. "I don't want to pry, Desta, but are you feeling homesick?"

Desta looked up from the notebook with a guarded expression on her face. "Homesick? Not at all," she said, her eyes shifting side to side as she spoke.

Nerissa's eyes narrowed. The girl was as bad at lying as Charis.

"Are you still angry with the twins?" Raysel persisted.

Desta squirmed uncomfortably. "No," she said quickly.

If she was anything like Charis, pressing her was unlikely to yield a straight answer, so Nerissa tried another angle. A little piece of her groaned inwardly, but if her instincts were right, this tactic would draw out the truth. "I think you *are* starting to pry, Raysel," she chided, and Desta gave her a grateful look. Nerissa smiled back gently and added, "Just know that you can talk to your 'older brother' about anything."

The grateful look slipped off Desta's face, and she pressed her lips together in a tight line. *Got you*, Nerissa thought. She had learned long ago that when the direct approach didn't work, guilt trips usually would. Wheedling probably wasn't the most honest method, but it was effective. Nerissa turned her attention back to the soup and watched out of the corner of her eye as Desta thumbed through the pages, flipping through them so quickly it was obvious she wasn't really reading.

A moment later, Desta came back to the table, notebook in hand. "I'm not homesick, but I really would like to send a message to my mother," she said.

"We should avoid contacting her unless it's absolutely necessary—in case Casimer's men are watching your village," Raysel said.

Desta's face fell. "I-I understand."

"Why do you want to contact her?" Nerissa asked. She shot an annoyed glance across the table at Raysel. They weren't going to find out what was going on by upsetting her, even if his answer was truthful. "The reason must have something to do with your notebook, right?"

"It does," Desta said slowly. "It started on the night those men attacked our camp at the hot springs."

"That was a frightening experience for you, I'm sure,"

Nerissa said soothingly. "Is it causing you to have nightmares?"

"No, not nightmares," Desta said, placing special emphasis on the last word.

"If not nightmares, then what?" Nerissa asked.

Desta took a deep breath, summoning up her courage. "This is going to sound strange because I don't have any of my mother's talent, but I had a prophetic dream right before the attack." The words tumbled from her lips in a rush as she recounted the dream she had right before the camp was attacked.

"I think you're mistaken on one thing for certain," Nerissa said when the explanation was finished. She patted Desta's hand comfortingly. "Apparently, you *do* have some of your mother's talent."

Desta gave her a wan smile. "Maybe I do. That's why I wanted to send her a message asking for advice. I know that my mother keeps a journal to record her dreams so that's why I bought a notebook as soon as I could. I've even made notes of older dreams when I can remember them. But I don't know how to tell the difference between normal dreams and meaningful ones. I would feel terrible if I got another warning and missed it. I'm sure my mother would be able to give me some guidance."

Raysel folded his napkin and laid it on the table. "Why didn't you tell us about the dream right away?"

"There was so much going on that night—and in the days immediately afterward. My dream didn't seem very important compared to watching out for the Senka. I wasn't sure what to think of it anyway. It might have been a coincidence or a one-time occurrence."

Raysel's head bobbed in understanding. "Tomorrow I'll be meeting with one of our contacts to see if any messages have been received from our village. I plan to send an update on our progress and inform them that we've lost our last contact in Silvus. What I said earlier about avoiding contact with Shae is still true. However, this is a special circumstance. If we send your message through our village, one of the Ohanzee messengers can deliver it to her without drawing attention. To do that, I'll need you to write your message to her tonight so I can take it with me first thing in the morning."

"I'll get started right away," Desta said. She practically bounded back to her bed to begin writing the letter, her smile finally reaching her eyes.

6

COMMONPLACE THINGS

Nerissa

The late morning breeze swept down from the mountains, carrying with it an icy tinge that hinted at the approach of winter. The people walking around Nerissa all rubbed their arms or pulled their cloaks tighter, but she was oblivious to the chill. She was already frozen in another way, her eyes fixated upward, riveted by the sight in front of her.

There, waving gently overhead, was a sight she had not seen anywhere else on their journey. Her grip tightened on the waxed paper bag until her knuckles turned white. The golden phoenix glinted in the sunlight as the crimson flag of Chiyo rippled against the cloudless sky. A part of her felt silly for being mesmerized by something as commonplace as the sight of Chiyo's flag. But it wasn't commonplace—not anymore. It had been conspicuously absent everywhere else or, worse, replaced by the dragon flag of Marise. Yet here it was in Rhea, boldly flying at full staff in the very center of the inner city—as it should be everywhere in Chiyo. And when she was through, it *would* be again.

She relaxed her grip on the bag and took a deep breath before continuing toward her destination. Alden likely kept the flag flying more as a symbol of defiance to Casimer than as a display of loyalty. Nerissa knew that, but it didn't alter the sense of pride she felt at seeing it again.

Nerissa weaved her way through the shoppers milling around the farmer's and artisan's stalls in the city square until she reached the hospital where Rian was being treated. She couldn't hold back her laughter when she saw that the tailor's shop next door to the hospital was called In Stitches. Still chuckling at the irony, she pushed open the door to the clinic and was immediately greeted by the pungent odor of antiseptics.

Aside from a bored-looking receptionist, the waiting room was empty. After a perfunctory reminder that morning visiting hours were nearing their end, the receptionist led her down a wide hallway neatly arrayed with carts carrying rolls of gauze, bottles, and other medical equipment.

The man stopped in front of a door about halfway down the hall and knocked once. "You have a visitor," he said as he opened the door.

Nerissa had taken no more than two steps inside before the man pulled the door closed behind her, clipping the back of her heel in the process. Apparently, the receptionist was in a hurry to return to his boredom.

Rian glanced up from the bed where he lie on his stomach, propped up on his elbows while reading a book. His open back shirt revealed the gauze dressings that covered from his shoulders to the bottom of his rib cage.

"Caeneus, I'm surprised to see you. Leal is finally feeling

better, so he and Jarold brought me breakfast. Even though the hospital food is nutritious, it's also terribly bland," he said, sticking his tongue out. "Jarold told me the twins plan to come by this afternoon, but he didn't say anything about you."

"That's because I didn't talk to them until after they came back," Nerissa said.

"That explains it." He closed the book he had been reading without bothering to mark the page and craned his neck to the side to see her better. "They weren't the only ones to visit this morning though. Raysel stopped by on his way to meet with one of our messengers. I told him you're not supposed to wake people when they are in the hospital, but he didn't care. Apparently, even injuries are no excuse to sleep in." Rian rolled his eyes melodramatically.

"That sounds like Raysel," Nerissa said, a slow grin spreading across her lips at the thought. "You're supposed to bring a gift whenever you visit someone in the hospital, so I have something for you." She handed him the bag she had brought with her and then took a seat in a chair next to the bed.

The paper crinkled as Rian peeked inside. He stuck his nose into the bag and inhaled deeply, his whole face lighting up in recognition. "Is this what I think it is?"

Nerissa's grin widened. "I remembered that you like cherry cobbler. It's my favorite too, after all. When I saw it was on the menu at the inn, I asked for a portion for you. The cook kindly made it ahead of time so I could bring it with me. It should still be warm, but if you're not hungry, you can always save it for later and send the container back with the twins."

"No, I'll eat it now! Cobbler tastes best when it's warm,"

Rian said excitedly. "I can't eat like this, though." He scooted to the edge of the bed and dropped his legs over the side. As he did so, the front of his shirt slid up, exposing a well-toned abdomen and a chest covered in gauze.

Nerissa felt heat rise to her cheeks, and she reflexively averted her gaze just like Raysel had done with her the night before. She realized too late that Caeneus would have no reason to turn away. When she looked again, Rian was sitting on the edge of the bed with a smirk. He had noticed her reaction.

Though she had gotten better at blending in with the other men, her guise always seemed to falter around Rian. Nerissa racked her brain to come up with a plausible reason for her response. "That looks awfully painful," she said as casually as she could.

"Do I have injuries on my stomach that I don't know about?" he asked.

"I meant that it looks like *moving* would be painful," she amended.

"I see. It still is, actually." Rian pulled the lid off the crock and dipped the accompanying spoon into the gooey treat. "This is almost as good as the sponge bath I got from the nurse last night," he said. A rakish grin spread across his lips as he spoke.

Nerissa's own smile evaporated, and she had to bite back the scathing comment that instantly leaped to her tongue. Instead, she muttered, "I bet," and forced out a choked laugh. It was a weak response, but it was the best she could muster under the circumstances.

Rian took another bite and chuckled like he was laughing at an inside joke. Nerissa fumed in silence while he enjoyed the next few bites. She was sure that Raysel would have chided him for making such a lecherous comment, but it seemed better for maintaining her disguise if she played along. Why did he have to say something like that right when she was starting to think fondly of him?

When Rian spoke again, his voice took on a serious tone. "The cuts must have looked bad yesterday, but the doctor said none of them are very deep. Aside from those, I have some bruises and soreness from being thrown into the wall. No head injury, fortunately. There's nothing that won't heal quickly with proper rest. I'll be released in a few days once they are sure that the wounds are healing well and no infection has settled in."

Nerissa's head hung in remorse. Whether she was irritated by his earlier comment or not, he was still here because he had been hurt on her behalf. "I am sincerely sorry that you were injured. I wasn't cautious enough, and it resulted in you being harmed."

Rian's spoon clattered against the rim of the ceramic crock. "How can you say that? You were the one who stopped the spirit. You stayed when I told you to go back without me, and you *carried* me out of the cave," Rian said, his voice bristling with disbelief.

"If I had been able to lift the strongbox on my own, the trap would never have been triggered," Nerissa argued.

"It wasn't possible to open it without taking it out of the chest first, and the box was very heavy. I'm not sure if I could have lifted it by myself either," Rian said.

"I don't know what you mean. There's no reason why I

65

shouldn't have been able to lift that box as readily as anyone else. I need to focus more on my training."

"I got hurt because our mission was dangerous, not because of some so-called shortcoming of yours. You're one of the strongest people I've ever met. That's one of the things I like about you."

Nerissa was reminded of when he said those same words to her in the cave, and her heartbeat picked up pace. She had disregarded the sentiment thinking that Rian was delirious at the time, but could he actually have been speaking the truth?

"I don't know what to think when you say things like that," she blurted out without thinking. As soon as the last word rolled off her tongue, she began mentally berating herself. How was she going to explain away her reaction? This was no time to misconstrue Rian's intentions or to hear in his words what she wished to hear. He saw her as Caeneus—a friend and comrade—and nothing more. The chair legs rasped across the floor as she jumped to her feet and turned so he wouldn't be able to see her face.

But, as it turned out, she hadn't misunderstood Rian's feelings. He lurched to his feet and seized her wrist, pulling her toward him.

"Finally, a crack shows in your facade," Rian said. "And I wasn't even trying to draw it out of you that time."

"Draw what out of me? W-what do you mean?" Nerissa stammered, unable to break away from his lazuline eyes.

"I know you're only pretending to be a man. I realized that a long time ago," Rian answered.

All hope of Nerissa salvaging her disguise vanished when

Rian lifted her hand and softly pressed his lips against the back of it. Her racing heart beat once in a single, resounding thump. Countless men had kissed her hand before—it was a commonplace, courtly greeting. Yet never before had one sent her senses reeling the way this one had. Its warmth lingered on her skin long after he withdrew.

Nerissa yanked her hand out of his grasp, even though it was the last thing she wanted to do. "That's absurd," she said, but she was too flustered to put any conviction behind the words.

"I don't know why you're pretending to be a man, and I don't know what you've done to change your voice. But I know you are a woman," Rian said. His words were earnest, emphatic. "Don't worry, I haven't told anyone, and I don't intend to tell anyone. I'll keep your secret. I'll *help* you keep your secret."

"How did you know?" Nerissa croaked. It was obvious that continuing to deny the truth would be pointless.

Rian's expression eased. "I met you on the night of the masquerade. You were wearing a mask so I couldn't see your face, but I would *never* forget your eyes."

The breath caught in Nerissa's throat at the inflection in his voice when he said "never." There was a tickle in the back of her mind, like a nebulous memory was floating just beyond reach. Though she struggled to find the connection, the feeling disappeared as quickly as it came.

Rian continued. "I recognized you again after our first sparring match. I deserved to taste the dirt for going all out on you like that, by the way. I knew those green eyes had to belong to you or a close relative. Since the Ohanzee women don't take part in training, I wasn't certain if you were really *you* or one of your siblings."

Nerissa squeezed her eyes closed as understanding dawned on her. "And then I told you I was an only child." He was sharp. What else had he managed to figure out about her?

"Exactly," Rian said. "You looked so shocked before. Did you really not suspect I discovered the truth about your disguise?"

Nerissa shook her head. "How could I possibly have known?"

"Didn't you wonder who put the bottle of perfume in your pocket?" he asked.

Nerissa's mouth fell open. The perfume...that had been a birthday gift from Raysel, hadn't it?

"When we were in Niamh, I passed by a perfumery, and the scent reminded me of the one you were wearing at the masquerade," Rian said. "I slipped it into your pocket when we stopped to reattach your prosthetics. You must have been surprised when you found the pouch, so I wondered why you never said anything about it."

"I really couldn't ask around without compromising my disguise, could I?"

"That's a good point, but I think there's more to it than that," Rian said slowly, his eyes narrowing as he watched her expression change. "I think someone else already knows your secret too."

Nerissa said nothing to confirm or deny his assertion, but it didn't matter.

"Raysel's your guardian. *He* knows. I've suspected that from the beginning," Rian asserted.

Nerissa sighed in defeat and rubbed her forehead. There didn't seem to be any reason to deny Raysel's involvement. "Yes, Raysel has known the whole time."

Rian nodded, satisfied. "There's one more thing I want to ask. What is your real name? It can't really be Caeneus."

He puzzled out all of that, but he still doesn't know who I really am, she thought. She couldn't remember anything about the day of the masquerade, but if he didn't know her name, they must have met after she changed costumes. Her chest ached with a longing to tell him, to have him know who she really was, but secrets were best kept by the fewest number of people possible.

Her lips twisted into a brittle smile. "If you know my real name, what is the point of a disguise?"

This time, it was Rian's face that took on a shocked expression. "The Chiefs said you lost your memories. Do you actually remember that night?"

Nerissa cocked her head in confusion. "I don't remember anything between going to bed the night before the masquerade and the time I woke up in Einar and Ildiko's house. What made you ask?"

"Your answer just now. That was almost the exact answer you gave me when I asked your name at the masquerade—" Rian answered.

A knock on the door cut Rian short, and a male nurse opened it a second later. "You shouldn't be out of bed," he scolded and, surprisingly, Rian dropped onto the edge of the mattress without protest. The nurse turned to Nerissa next and said, "Visiting hours are over."

"Don't forget to take this back with you," Rian said, holding out the bag with the now empty crock inside. When Nerissa reached out to take it, Rian whispered in her ear. "Remember when I said I had been trying to draw the truth out of you? *He's* my nurse. I made the sponge bath comment earlier to try to get you riled up enough to give yourself away."

Nerissa glared at him, but Rian simply smirked up at her with a twinkle in his eyes. "As soon as you are better I am going to make you pay for that," she hissed.

The same rakish grin from before spread across Rian's face again. "I hope so," he said as she was ushered from the room.

Their conversation would have to be continued later, but Nerissa wasn't sure if she should look forward to it or dread it. As much as he may be able to tell her about the night of the masquerade, she also knew he wouldn't give up on trying to puzzle out her true identity.

And she wasn't sure that she truly wanted to keep it from him anymore either.

7

THORN OF THE WHITE ROSE

Raysel

A bell jangled overhead as Raysel stepped into the luthier's shop. There was no sign of the instrument maker amid the violins and other stringed instruments on display, nor behind the counter where bows, strings, and bags of rosin hung in neat rows. He was pleased to find that the shop was empty of other customers as well.

Gasparo, the proprietor, was one of several Ohanzee informants in Rhea. Raysel made a point of casually browsing the violins while he waited to be greeted. Until he knew whether it was Gasparo or one of his employees working today, it was best to maintain the appearance of a customer. His eyes wandered to the window where he could see a constant stream of passersby. Who could say whether or not there were curious eyes among the milling crowd? Though he was always cautious, Brigs' recent betrayal had elevated Raysel's sense of suspicion to an entirely new level.

Just as his patience was beginning to wear thin, a gray-

71

haired man pushed aside the curtain separating the shop from the workroom.

"How may I help you?" the man asked tersely, peering at Raysel over the top of his glasses.

"Are you Gasparo?" Raysel asked.

The man nodded once and raised his eyebrows impatiently.

"I'm here to pick up a violin for my band leader. He sent it here to be restrung and to have the scroll replaced."

Gasparo's attitude changed abruptly. His brow creased, and he spoke slowly as if searching for the right words to say. "Yes, and I believe he also sent four bows to be rehaired, did he not?"

"With only the finest stallion hair," Raysel confirmed.

Gasparo rubbed his hands together and stared at Raysel's sword in awe. Then he strode over to the door, locked it, and dropped a closed sign in the window. "It's been many years since I've met with one of the Ohanzee in person. For a moment, I worried I had forgotten the code phrase," he said.

"Can we speak somewhere more private?" Raysel asked, directing a pointed look at the shopfront window.

"Of course! Of course! No one else is here now, but please follow me. There are no windows back here." Gasparo parted the curtain leading to the workroom and gestured for Raysel to enter.

"Have you received any recent communications from the Ohanzee?" Raysel asked once the curtain dropped into place behind them.

"Indeed, I have. Both letters arrived yesterday, in fact," Gasparo said.

"Both? There was more than one?"

Gasparo nodded in affirmation. "One came sealed, bearing instructions to burn it after two weeks. The other was addressed directly to me, which was a bit baffling. I'm glad you're here because I'm not quite sure what to make of it. It's written as if it were from a distant relative of mine who lives in Marise, but I don't have any relatives living outside of Chiyo." He went to the fireplace and pulled one of the bricks out of place. Behind it was an empty space just large enough to store the letters and a handful of small trinkets.

Now, Raysel's curiosity piqued. "I will begin with that letter if you don't mind." He took both envelopes and skimmed the contents of the one addressed to Gasparo first.

The letter did, indeed, give the impression of being from a distant relative in Nyx, the capital city of Marise, but Raysel recognized the neat, precise handwriting as Ildiko's. The opening lines carried customary greetings, generic commentary on the weather, and updates on the activities of various— apparently fictional—nieces and nephews.

Raysel shared Gasparo's confusion about the letter's purpose until he reached the bottom. The very last paragraph mentioned that an illness had begun to spread through Nyx. It detailed the symptoms and lamented that the sickness seemed to be resistant to the modern medicines commonly used by Marisianne doctors. Fortunately, an alternative treatment had been found that was suitably effective. The letter went on to describe ingredients for the remedy and suggested it would be wise to keep the concoction on hand in case the illness eventually reached Rhea.

Very clever, Ildiko, Raysel thought.

"The point of this letter is to disseminate the cure for a disease that is spreading through Marise without revealing the information came from the Ohanzee," he said, handing the letter back to Gasparo. "Play along with the story that this is from a distant relative, and see to it that these instructions are distributed to all the practitioners of medicine in the city. If the illness ever does spread to Rhea, your doctors will be well prepared."

"How ingenious," Gasparo said. "I will do as you say immediately."

"I appreciate your eagerness, but be careful not to call attention to yourself in your haste. The illness hasn't made its way here yet, so you can afford to share the information discreetly."

"Of course," Gasparo agreed.

Raysel smirked. He was beginning to think that "of course" might be Gasparo's favorite thing to say. Turning his attention to the second envelope, he lifted the seal with his thumb and withdrew the paper inside. The message, this time in Hania's purposeful but shaky strokes, confirmed what he already suspected. Ildiko had been able to find an appropriate cure from within the medical texts housed in the Archives. The cure's effectiveness had already been verified by successful treatment of some patients in Niamh with symptoms similar to those described in the prophecy. Hania was now using his network of contacts to distribute Ildiko's instructions throughout Chiyo.

There was a postscript at the bottom where Hania's writing became tightly spaced and uneven, giving the appearance that the lines had been added in a hurry. It advised that they acquire the ingredients for the remedy as soon as possible and add them to the medical kit Ildiko had sent with them. Raysel chuckled inwardly. There was no doubt in his mind that Ildiko had been impatiently hovering over Hania's shoulder dictating what to write.

Gasparo eyed him curiously as he folded the paper and returned it to the envelope, but Raysel felt no need to divulge anything about the contents. He slipped the letter into a pocket sewn into the inner lining of his vest and withdrew the two envelopes he brought with him. "Both of these should be sent back to the village at the first opportunity."

"That won't be a problem," Gasparo said. "I'll send a pigeon this afternoon to summon the designated courier."

Having concluded his business with Gasparo, Raysel stepped out from the side street into the city square. Since his path took him past the hospital, he briefly considered stopping in to see Rian again, but one glance at the clock tower told him that morning visiting hours had recently ended. Unlike Gasparo's shop, the businesses here in the city square were bustling with customers. Raysel meandered down the sidewalk, matching his pace with those walking around him. He couldn't resist chuckling to himself as he walked under the sign for In Stitches, the tailor shop located next to the hospital. Just then, the hospital door swung open and a familiar figure emerged.

"Caeneus!" he called out, but Nerissa was too far ahead to

hear him over the clamor of the square.

Raysel picked up his pace, effortlessly dodging through the crowd until he reached her. "Caeneus," he said again at the same time that she turned to see who had approached. He was surprised to see a pensive expression on her face, but it quickly lightened at the sight of him. "I didn't know you were planning to go out this morning."

"Raysel, I'm glad to see you," Nerissa said. "I decided to pay Rian a visit, and I brought him some cherry cobbler." She held up the bag in her hand for him to see.

"Is Rian alright? You look a little shaken."

She tilted her head to the side and drew a deep breath. "I suppose I am a little shaken but not because of Rian. Or perhaps I should say that it's not because there is anything *wrong* with Rian."

Raysel's brow creased. "Could you be more cryptic? I can almost understand what you're trying to say."

Nerissa responded by sniffing and giving him a wry look. "You didn't give me a bottle of perfume for my birthday, did you?" she asked.

"A bottle of perfume? No, I gave you two of Pan's pastries," he answered.

"*Just* the pastries?" she persisted.

"Yes, just the pastries," he said, feeling surprised and a little hurt that she didn't remember the gifts clearly. While the present certainly hadn't been expensive, he thought it would hold sentimental value for her. "That's why I didn't want you to share one with me. I didn't want to eat half of your gift. How are the pastries related to Rian?"

"I'm getting to that," Nerissa answered. "I found two gifts in the pocket of my cloak on my birthday: the two pastries and a bottle of strawberry and rose scented perfume."

Raysel stopped short. He reached out, taking Nerissa's upper arm and pulling her to a stop as well. "The scent that you used to wear every day?"

"More specifically, the one I wore to the masquerade," Nerissa said. "I thought the bottle had also been from you, but I found out it was actually from Rian."

"So he knows…," Raysel let his voice trail off, afraid to say anything more in public.

"He said that we met at the masquerade, and he recognized me when we met again during our first sparring match," Nerissa explained.

A woman bumped into Raysel's shoulder as she passed by carrying a bushel of potatoes. She called out an apology, but the incident was enough to make Raysel worry that they may be drawing attention. "Let's keep walking as we talk, and be careful what you say," he advised. Nerissa nodded in agreement. Resuming where he left off before being interrupted, he said, "If he gave you a birthday present, he must know who you are."

"He told me he passed by a perfumery in Niamh and happened to recognize the scent. I don't think the gift was related to my birthday at all."

Birthday present or not, the fact that he stopped and bought it for you is significant on its own, Raysel thought, but he didn't say it out loud. Rian had given girls flowers before, but he had never bought any of them a gift. That he had bought perfume for

Nerissa, even if it was a spontaneous decision—perhaps *especially* if it was a spontaneous decision—spoke volumes about his feelings for her.

For Raysel, it was an oddly bittersweet realization. Despite the fact that it was a part of his duty, he had felt guilty for not being able to tell Rian that Caeneus was actually the girl he had danced with at the masquerade. Now, since Rian had discovered the truth on his own, there was no need for Raysel to hide his knowledge of it any longer. But at the same time, he felt oddly envious of his friend. Rian was free to act on his feelings for Nerissa—if he wanted to. Even though Raysel knew from the start that relationships between the Royal Family and their personal guardians were forbidden, never before had having Thorn at his side felt so much like having a thorn *in* his side. There was no way he would ever give voice to those thoughts, however.

Nerissa eyed him curiously, and he realized he must have been preoccupied with his thoughts for too long. Raysel quickly formulated a response to her earlier comment. "Sorry, I was wondering when and how Rian figured everything out. Did he tell you?"

Nerissa explained how Rian had slowly pieced the clues together and that he had also figured out Raysel was in on the secret the whole time.

"I admit, this news comes as somewhat of a relief. Rian is reliable, and it will make things easier on both of us to have an additional ally," Raysel said. They rounded the street corner, and the inn they were staying at finally came into view.

"He still doesn't know who I am," Nerissa said, and the pensive look from earlier returned to her face. "But I wonder how long it will be before he figures that out too?"

Just then, a child carrying a basket of freshly cut roses approached them. "Would either of you gentlemen like to buy a flower for your ladies?" the boy asked in a clearly rehearsed tone of voice. "Only two gold per stem."

Raysel opened his mouth to decline, but Nerissa's hand was in her pocket.

"I'll take one," she said, pressing a five gold coin into the boy's palm.

He handed her a rose and began to count out her change, but she stopped him with a wave of her hand. "There's no need for that. Tell your parents the extra is meant to be a reward for your hard work," she said.

The boy's eyes grew twice their size, and his mouth fell open. "Thank you!" he said, practically shouting with excitement.

"I think you made his day," Raysel said, grinning as the boy scurried away.

Nerissa twirled the white rose, admiring the blossom for a moment before burying her nose in it. "My mother said generosity rewards the giver as much as it does the receiver. Three gold is a small sum, but it's a huge amount to a child." She paused to inhale the aroma again. "Besides, I have a soft spot for white roses. How could I resist?"

A bittersweet feeling crept back into Raysel's chest as he opened the door leading to the lobby of the inn. It was both his duty and his honor to protect Nerissa, and she had made it abundantly clear from the start that she did not want others to make sacrifices for her sake. She deserved a partner who would make her happy, and having a loved one die protecting her would definitely *not* make her happy. As long as he was willing to lay down his life for her safety—and he would always be willing to do so, no matter what she said—he would never be able to be that person for her. As her personal guardian, he was never *meant* to be that person for her. He grasped Thorn's hilt, and the weight that had invaded his chest began to lighten. No matter what the nature of their relationship was, he would always be the sword by her side.

8

UNEXPECTED CONNECTIONS

Nerissa

Raysel stepped across the threshold into the inn's lobby and immediately stopped short. Nerissa, following one step behind him, quickly hopped to one side to avoid colliding with his back. Before she could ask what was going on, the answer to her question became clear. There, standing in front of the inn's ornate fireplace mantle, was Alden.

"Here are two of the people I've been waiting for!" he exclaimed, reaching out to shake hands in greeting. Nerissa was not at all surprised to see Kuma's head sticking out of the satchel slung across his chest. At this point, she would have been shocked to see Alden without Kuma nearby.

"You've been waiting for us?" Raysel asked skeptically, finally stepping out of the doorway to take Alden's hand.

"Well, not the two of you specifically. It seems that your patrons, Jarold and Leal, have gone out for lunch."

Seeing Raysel's furrowed brow, Alden cast a pointed look

in the direction of the desk clerk and then shot her a disarming smile when their eyes met. The woman fluttered her eyelashes and responded with a radiant smile of her own. "I came to inquire about the antiques we discussed the other day. Although I have been enjoying the welcome provided to me by the inn's attentive staff, I don't have much more time to wait for your patrons to return. I realize the two of you are employed as merchants' guards, not assistants, but could you show me the items in their stead?"

Nerissa knew that Alden didn't really have any business with Jarold and Leal, so the elaborate cover story must be for the benefit of those around them. The woman at the desk wasn't even attempting to hide the fact that she was listening in on their conversation.

"I am sure they would want us to accommodate you. Why don't you come to our room where we can conduct our business in private," Nerissa suggested.

"I'll have room service bring up a complimentary tea tray and some snacks in a few minutes," the desk clerk chimed in.

"That would be delightful," Alden replied smoothly. If the woman's overt eavesdropping bothered him, he didn't let it show.

The clerk bowed her head politely and said, "It is a pleasure to share our inn's hospitality with you, Governor Alden."

"Would you also be kind enough to return this to the kitchen and send up a vase with the tea tray?" Nerissa asked, sliding the bag containing the empty cobbler crock across the counter and holding up the rose so the woman could see it.

"I will see to it personally," the clerk said absently, her eyes still glued to Alden.

———◆———

The staircase leading to the third floor was every bit as opulent as the rest of the inn. With its carved mahogany handrails and marble-topped steps, it would easily have rivaled the grand staircase in the Manor—if the Manor were still standing. Nerissa trailed absent-mindedly behind Raysel and Alden as they climbed to the third floor, her thoughts consumed by the earlier conversation with Rian. She was so preoccupied that she almost didn't notice the clatter that arose from within their room the moment Raysel pushed the door open.

"Caeneus, Raysel! I think I've found a connection between the books!" Desta proclaimed, bounding toward them from across the room. Her expression rapidly transformed from elation to chagrin as the door swung open to reveal Alden's presence as well. "I-I-I didn't know someone else was with you," she stammered.

Nerissa sighed and gave her a withering look. They were going to have a talk about behaving rashly later, but it couldn't be helped now. After all, spilled milk could not be returned to its glass. If they put off discussing Desta's findings, they would offend Alden, and the last thing they needed to do was alienate one of their few allies.

It seemed Raysel came to the same conclusion. He checked to be sure the hall was empty and then closed the door. "Desta, I don't believe that you've met Governor Alden before."

Desta stared down at her feet regretfully. She glanced up only long enough to greet Alden before casting them downward again. Kuma emitted a soft "arf," and Nerissa saw that the dog had gone rigid, seemingly mesmerized by Desta.

"Alden already knows about our search for the books," Raysel explained. "So you may as well tell us what kind of connection you think you've found."

Desta touched her index fingers together in a nervous gesture and pursed her lips. "When my mother and I snuck into the University Library, we weren't able to find any other books with crystals in their spines. Since looking for the crystals seemed to be a dead end, I thought the cover designs might share a common link. Then we met Caeneus, and I completely forgot about the idea until this afternoon. There was something about the pattern on the front of the newest book that seemed familiar, so I decided to take another look at it while the twins were on duty guarding the wagon. I've figured out what caught my eye. There *is* an element of the design that all three books have in common."

"What element is that?" Nerissa asked.

Desta scurried to the table to retrieve the book. She pointed to the diamond and triangle on the front. "All of them have triangles on their covers."

"Triangles? Desta, that's a really common shape," Raysel said. "I doubt it's significant that there is one on all three covers."

Though Nerissa shared Raysel's skepticism, she saw the gleam of recognition in Alden's eyes as he looked at the design. The book had been inside the cave all of Alden's life, so this must be his first time seeing it. Yet something about its appearance was plainly familiar to him.

"I know triangles are common shapes," Desta said, flipping her hair over one shoulder peevishly. "That's not all there is to it. This book has four triangles on the cover, and it contains the fourth section of the prophecy. The one we got from Charis has three triangles on the cover, and it contains the third section of the prophecy."

"And your mother's?" Nerissa prompted. She couldn't remember what the cover of Shae's book looked like, but she knew Desta would.

Desta smiled gratefully. "I can't show it to you since we don't have it with us, but I would never forget what it looks like. My mother's family seal was stamped into the leather. The design is a collage of many symbols that represent her family arranged into the overall shape of a triangle."

"Even though triangles may be a common element in designs, the correlation between the number of them on the cover and the section of the prophecy the book contains has to be intentional," Nerissa said.

Alden stepped forward and thrust his right hand in front of them. He wiggled his ring finger, calling attention to the large gold band he wore. "I think there's another, less obvious connection too. That isn't just a random grouping of four triangles. It's *my* family's crest."

Nerissa, Raysel, and Desta leaned forward in unison to better see the insignia on his ring. Sure enough, it was a perfect match with the book cover's central design.

"I suppose it would make sense for the family crests to match the covers since all of the books we've found so far have been heirlooms," Raysel said.

Nerissa snapped her fingers as realization dawned on her. For once, she felt grateful for the countless hours of history lessons she had taken. "The first book said the prophecy was recorded and hidden during King Gared's time. One of his most famous decrees was the implementation of a system for individuals and businesses to use unique crests. Although we don't use them for their original purpose anymore, back then the crests were used to authorize financial transactions in place of gold. The practice was highly effective in deterring banditry and thievery because travelers and merchants didn't need to carry money with them," Nerissa said.

Noticing that Desta's and Alden's eyes were starting to glaze over, she jumped to the point. "Since both the books and crests would have been created around the same time period, it isn't too far-fetched to think that the original owners might have incorporated a subtle reference to the prophecy in their family crests."

"That's a good theory. A triangle motif is common enough that it wouldn't be easy to track the books and owners using that information alone," Raysel agreed.

"You've made an excellent discovery, Desta. We should be able to use this information to help pinpoint who to approach during our search," Nerissa said, and Desta beamed with pride.

Alden cleared his throat. "I realize you would have preferred not to discuss this revelation in my presence, but Desta's impulsiveness may actually have done you a favor."

"How so?" Raysel asked.

"Do you remember what I told you about my great-grandfather's friend Barr?"

"The 300-year-old expert on crystals that helped set the trap in the cave?" Raysel replied. He didn't try to hide the hint of disbelief that colored his tone. "A story like that is hard to forget."

"Yes, him," Alden said. "I honestly don't know how much truth there is in my great-grandfather's tales, but considering what happened in the cave, there must be *something* to them." There was no need for him to elaborate further. The events of the previous day were fresh enough that everyone in the room knew what he meant. "It so happens that Barr's family crest has two triangles included in its design. He and my great-grandfather exchanged letters for many years after he moved back to Marise, so I've seen his seal on the old envelopes. It may only be a coincidence, but it would probably be a worthwhile place to resume your search. Even though Barr must have passed away decades ago, someone in the village is bound to know his heirs."

"And his address must be on those old letters," Nerissa surmised.

"Yes, he lived in Kisoji. It's a very old village in the northern mountains just across the border in Marise," Alden replied.

Raysel sighed unexpectedly. "That certainly is valuable information, but it brings us back to a problem we've been ignoring until now." He paused as a knock came from the hall door.

A cheerful voice sang out, "Room service."

87

"That must be your tea," Raysel said with a wry smile.

Alden shrugged noncommittally. "She would have been offended if I refused her offer. Governing does have a few perks."

Raysel shook his head, opened the door, and invited the room service attendant inside. The woman wheeled in a cart overflowing with finger sandwiches, cookies, and scones. It was quite an impressive array of teas and treats—almost ridiculously so. There was even a small plate with a bone-shaped cookie on it for Kuma. Desta watched the cart roll by with a ravenous look in her eyes. But no matter how delicious the food appeared, it would have to wait until their discussion was finished. Nerissa took the intermission as an opportunity to consider the problem Raysel had referred to.

The attendant departed after repeatedly informing them that she would return promptly should they need anything more. Nerissa waited until the door closed again before saying, "The problem you were referring to is that the Senka will be watching both of the drawbridges. There's no way for us to leave Rhea without confronting them, right?"

"Exactly," Raysel said. "By the time Rian is ready to leave the hospital, the Senka will have had ample time to discover their operatives are missing and have reinforcements on their way. They will undoubtedly outnumber us. We could call in reinforcements of our own, but a direct confrontation could be costly. If possible, we need to find a way to leave the region undercover."

Alden scrunched up his nose, and the tiny bells in his hair jingled as he scratched his head. "I believe I may also be able to offer a solution to that problem. It's actually one of the reasons I came here today. The last thing I want is to draw Casimer's attention by having a skirmish take place between you and the Senka on my border."

"What kind of solution did you have in mind?" Nerissa asked.

"There's a third bridge, though it doesn't span the Yoshie River. It crosses the Ameles on the far northern and eastern border of Rhea instead."

"A third bridge?" Raysel asked. "I've never seen a map that showed a bridge across the Ameles."

"I'm sure you wouldn't have. A wise man never reveals all of his secrets, especially when he is in a position of power." Alden directed a cryptic smile at Nerissa. "Wouldn't you agree, Caeneus?"

"Naturally. It's a wise practice in both business and politics," she replied, deliberately keeping her expression neutral. There was no reason to think he harbored any specific suspicions. Still, her disguise had already been compromised once today. She didn't intend on letting it happen again.

"I should warn you—the bridge is very old and hasn't been maintained for decades," Alden continued. "You should use caution when crossing because it may not be in good condition. On the other hand, it's actually part of a defunct trade route that used to connect Rhea and Kisoji, so it provides you with a convenient shortcut to Barr's village."

"And you can provide us with a map that actually *does* show its location?" Raysel asked.

Alden waved his hand and then patted Kuma's head. The dog was straining to lean closer to the cart, his nose quivering as he sniffed the air. "Of course, I will. There's no point in telling you about the bridge and then not telling you where to find it. I don't want to alienate one of my few allies."

Hearing Alden so closely echo her own sentiments made Nerissa smile. "You said the bridge was one of your reasons for coming today. What was the other?"

"I had two others, actually. First I wanted to see the book. Since we left the cave in a hurry due to Rian's injuries, there was no time for me to look at it yesterday. It's been hidden in the cave my whole life, so I wanted to see it at least once before parting with it. If you don't mind, perhaps I could look it over while we enjoy our refreshments."

Nerissa nodded her assent, and Alden went on without pause. "The last reason is that I wanted to give you this." He reached into his pocket and pulled something out. "I don't know whether or not you will need this in the future, but I thought you should have it."

He placed the crystal fragment in Nerissa's outstretched palm, and it glowed softly. "Thank you, Alden. I'll keep it with the piece that was in the book."

"Good, they are meant to be together. Consider it a symbol of our alliance," Alden said, and Nerissa couldn't help but smile again.

"Since we have enough food here to last for days, there's no reason for you to hurry as you look over the book," she said.

Alden lifted Kuma from his pouch and placed him on the floor. The dog's legs were already in motion before they touched the carpet. Instead of running to the cart as expected, he went straight to Desta and pawed at her shins. She looked down in surprise and then picked him up, giggling as Kuma covered her face with a barrage of licks.

Alden watched the interaction with his jaw hanging open. "Whose dog are you anyway?" he asked.

Nerissa was sure that he meant it to sound like a joke, but she could hear an underlying hint of jealousy too. "I guess this is our chance to take the best sweets for ourselves," she suggested with a wink.

Alden chuckled. He took the plate with the bone, placed it on the floor, and then sat down at the table. "It would be a shame to let the cooks' hard work go to waste."

"I couldn't agree more," Nerissa said before popping the first of many pastries into her mouth.

9

THE DRAGON'S MARK

Echidna

Echidna withdrew her finger from the soil and promptly wiped it clean on the lace-edged cloth offered by her handmaid. Although she loathed the feeling of dirt caked beneath her long fingernail, it was a small sacrifice to ensure her precious orchids were properly cared for. Normally, menial labor such as gardening would be beneath her, but these were orchids—the queen of all flowers.

She didn't care that roses were often referred to as the queen of all flowers. That was simply because orchids were so rare that most commoners had never laid eyes upon one. Their vivid colors and exotically shaped petals exposed roses as the glorified weeds they were. Orchids were not flowers that could be raised by just anyone. She had toiled over these plants since long before Ladon was born, waiting five years before the first luscious bloom could be coaxed out. After investing so much time, there was no way she would entrust their care to a maid who might be too generous or too stingy with the watering can.

"Mother, I'm bored," Ladon whined. "I want to go outside to play. Why can't I play with my friends anymore?" He gazed up at her with imploring blue eyes.

"Now, now, my Prince, you shouldn't bother your mother while she tends her flowers," his nanny chided gently. She picked up a wooden horse and trotted it across the blanket in front of him. "There's no reason to be bored. You have armloads of toys to play with right here."

Ladon slapped the horse from her hand. "I want to play outside!" he screeched and then rolled onto his back, pummeling his arms and legs against the ground, sending toys scattering in every direction. He flailed around so much that one of his shoes flew off into a flower pot. His shirt came untucked and rode up to expose the dragon outline that had been tattooed over his heart shortly after birth, marking him as the heir to the throne.

"Ladon! Whining and bleating to get your way is not behavior befitting a prince," Echidna scolded, eyes blazing.

Ladon stopped thrashing and jutted out his bottom lip sullenly. "I want to go outside!"

"My Queen, please don't be too hard on him," the nanny pleaded. "Being cooped up and isolated like this is hard on everyone, but it must be particularly difficult for an active young boy like the prince."

Echidna arched one perfectly sculpted eyebrow. "Oh, I see. Well, if it means that much to you, do as you wish, Ladon," she purred sweetly.

Ladon jumped to his feet and scurried to the greenhouse door. He jiggled the handle in a futile effort, unable to lift the latch himself.

Echidna ignored his attempts to open the door and spoke as if she were addressing the nanny. "After all, I will love my darling son no matter what he does. If it turns out that he is incapable of obeying his dear mother's instructions, perhaps his father will decide to adopt a new tradition. We could *choose* who will inherit the throne like they used to do in Chiyo. The country might not have been entirely backward after all."

Ladon whirled around and rushed to his mother, pressing his face into her voluminous skirts. "No! I can listen. I'll be a good prince from now on. I promise!"

She patted his black curls. "I believe you. You do understand why you can't go out to play with your friends, don't you?"

"Yes," Ladon answered, his voice muffled by fabric. "Everyone is getting sick, and I have to stay inside away from others so I don't get sick too."

"That's right, darling. I know it's difficult, but be patient. Your father is working hard to make the illness go away. You shouldn't have to wait much longer." A long-suffering sigh escaped Echidna's lips as Ladon sniffled in response and rubbed his nose on her skirt.

Just then, one of the doors to the greenhouse opened and another of Echidna's handmaids appeared. She bobbed a deep curtsy before speaking. "My Queen, you asked me to inform you when the king's guests arrived."

"They are rather early for their meeting, aren't they? Then again, I suppose a degree of overzealousness is to be expected from a common printer shop owner upon being summoned to the king."

The handmaid stared down at the floor. "It seems their meeting time was moved up by an hour. Somehow the change was not noted on your schedule for the day, so I have just learned of it. They are with him in the throne room as we speak."

Echidna exhaled one long, slow breath and peeled Ladon away from her skirts. "I should be on my way immediately," she said. She carefully controlled her tone of voice to make certain her annoyance didn't show, but inside she was fuming.

She straightened her skirts and checked her hair in the compact mirror offered by her handmaid. Nils had tried to convince her that her presence was not necessary at this meeting, despite her own insistence on attending. And now the schedule had been *conveniently* changed without notice. She snapped the cover of the mirror closed and flounced out the door.

"Open the doors," Echidna commanded as soon as her slippers touched the blue carpet that lead into the throne room.

The footmen hastened to obey, but she was forced to stop short when the doors swung open from the other side. The printer and his wife emerged, and Echidna could see that every inch of their exposed skin was mottled with black splotches—even their faces. Ink, if her guess was right. *How dare they not bathe properly before presenting themselves to their king,* she thought. She took a deep breath to cool her temper and decided to give them the benefit of the doubt. Perhaps the ink had sunken so deeply into their skin that no amount of soap could remove it.

The woman was the first to spot Echidna, and she nearly tripped over her own two feet in an awestruck attempt to curtsy. When she hesitantly lifted her eyes to offer a buck-toothed smile to her queen, the ends of the fabric hairband she wore drooped forward into her face. Embarrassed, she flicked her head, and the cloth flopped over her ears instead.

Echidna bowed her head ever so slightly in acknowledgement and folded her hands in front of her. Layers of silk from her long sleeves flowed down, draping the multitude of rings and bracelets she wore in a sheer curtain. The woman's cheeks turned pink, and then she and her husband were ushered away by the servant escorting them.

Echidna stepped into the throne room, and the doors closed behind her with a resounding thud. The blue carpet she walked on spanned the room and undulated up the stairs to where her husband sat poised on the dais. The silver Dragon Crown decorated his brow, as it always did when he entertained an audience, and a thick book lay across his knees.

"I want you to send ten guards to watch their home," Casimer said to Nils. "If the Ohanzee are seeking these books, they are bound to make an appearance there eventually. I want your men to intercept them and seize their possessions when they do. Use whatever means necessary."

Nils bowed, pressing his hand to his heart. "That will be problematic, my King. My men have already been spread thin. We have already deployed groups to observe travelers in and out of both Rhea and Silvus. We have also increased the number of patrols in Niamh and assigned additional men to monitor the spread of the illness through Marise."

"Don't you mean *my* men," Casimer corrected. "I am sure you can muster ten more able bodies for this task. See that it is done."

"Yes, my King."

First he doesn't inform me of the schedule change, and now he quibbles over my husband's command? Echidna thought.

She stepped forward, making a point to ignore Nil's presence. "I am sorry to have missed your guests, darling. I was not made aware that the meeting time had been changed."

"An unfortunate oversight," Nils interjected.

"Make sure it does not happen again," Casimer replied absently, distracted by his examination of the tome in his hands.

Nils bowed. "As you wish."

Casimer fanned through the book's pages. "Come and look this over with me, dear wife. I can find nothing particularly special about it aside from the crystal in its spine. You have sharp eyes. Perhaps you'll see something I do not."

Echidna lifted her skirts to climb the stairs and settled herself on the arm of Casimer's throne. "I've never heard of books being embellished with crystals, although I must say that I like the idea. Everything is improved by a bit of decoration." She plucked the crystal from the spine and held it in a shaft of light streaming through the window. It was pretty but nothing more than an ordinary rock.

Casimer chuckled. "Somehow hearing that answer from you is not surprising. Still, if the Ohanzee are searching for these, they must hold some sort of significance. Your idea to send inquiries to the registered printing houses within Marise was an excellent one."

"Aside from libraries, printers' master copies represent the largest collections of books," Echidna said with a self-satisfied smile.

"Even so, out of all the printers in Marise, only one possessed a book with a crystal in its spine. It wasn't among their master copies either. They said it was a family heirloom."

"They truly are loyal subjects to be willing to surrender something so precious to their king."

"Indeed. And yet we don't know the books' significance. How are we to know if this is one of those the Ohanzee are searching for?" Casimer asked, flipping through the pages once again. "It's a collection of old stories—the kind every child knows by the time they reach Ladon's age."

Echidna tapped one finger against her cheek. "Perhaps it is not the content that is important but something about the book itself. May I have a closer look?"

"Please do," Casimer said as he passed it over to her. "In the meantime, Nils, I would like an update on the illness afflicting my people."

Echidna held the book beneath her nose and then snorted softly to expel the scent of moldering paper. There was nothing extraordinary about its smell other than its stench.

Nils stepped closer to the dais and knelt. "Unfortunately, the sickness continues to spread and remains as virulent as ever. However, we have received word that doctors in Niamh have begun circulating an herb-based cure."

"Herbs?" Casimer scoffed. "Am I to believe that plants can cure an illness our modern medicines can't?"

Echidna looked up from her inspection of the book and laughed behind one hand. "If that were the case, one could avoid ever getting sick by eating an apple every day."

"I merely report what I have learned and let you judge its value," Nils said. "If you so choose, I can have one of my men acquire the recipe for its preparation."

"That will not be necessary," Casimer replied. "As you said earlier, we have limited resources and need to reserve our efforts for endeavors that will produce useful results."

A sneer spread across Echidna's lips, but she remained silent. She ran her fingers down the book's spine and into the pocket the stone came out of. Finding nothing remarkable, she opened the cover and idly traced her fingernails along the edge of the fabric lining the inner cover.

"I think that is a wise choice, my King." Nils shifted his weight, clearly uncomfortable kneeling despite the cushioning from the plush carpet. "Might I suggest you consider sending the prince to your country estate to better shield him from this sickness? After all, he is your only heir."

"Though it would pain me to be separated from him, it may be best to send him away until we find a cure—particularly since children are among the most severely affected."

Echidna's finger twitched so sharply her nail snagged the edge of the lining. The aging adhesive let loose easily, and the corner of the fabric peeled away. "No, you will not send him away!"

Casimer laid his hand over hers. "You know as well as I do that he is terribly unhappy being confined inside the castle. The sickness hasn't spread to the regions around our country estate yet. Ladon would be free to do as he liked."

"Then you need to pursue the potential cure from Niamh. You can't send your son away until you've exhausted all of your options!" Echidna's nails bit into her palm, but she did not loosen her fists.

"You're trembling, my dear," Casimer said, patting her hand consolingly. "If it upsets you so much, I will take some time to consider what is best for our family." His eyes drifted away from her face and down to the book. "What is that?"

Echidna followed his gaze to where the fabric covering had been torn away. Scripted words in black ink scrolled across the exposed area and disappeared beneath the cloth. She grabbed the corner, pulling it away until the whole page was uncovered.

> The fifth section of the prophecy is as follows:
>
> The attempt is ill-fated, however. Entering the presence of the Destroyer will put the Reflection in grave peril, and he will spill their blood a second time.
>
> The Destroyer's reign will be brought to an end by one who bears the dragon's mark, but the sword that pierces his heart will not be wielded in malice. In his absence, the Revenant will seize the empty throne.

"It's a prophecy," Echidna said in barely more than a whisper.

Casimer jabbed at the text with his index finger. "This must be why the Ohanzee are searching for these books."

Nils was hovering behind the throne, reading over their shoulders before Echidna realized he had moved. "It says this is the fifth section. It will be challenging to interpret the meaning without having all of the sections."

Casimer's voice was filled with scorn. "I put no stock in superstitions like prophecies. The only way to predict the future is through the study of past events and patterns. You should know I find there is no truth to be derived from fancies and dreams, Nils."

Nils pressed his lips together in a tight line. "I know that fact well, my King. I was not making reference to your ability to interpret the prophecy. I was pointing out that having this in our possession hinders *theirs*."

"Fair enough. I may not believe in this nonsense, but our enemies do."

"Still, what harm is there in giving this prophecy a small degree of consideration?" Echidna asked. "If the Ohanzee seek the books to obtain all of its pieces, they must view it as a way to help them avenge their fallen rulers. I don't see any other reason why they would be collecting them. Even if it is untrue, studying this section may provide some clues about our enemies' plans."

"When you put it that way, it does make sense to use the text to gather more insight. Yet how are we to know who the Destroyer, the Reflection, and the Revenant are?"

"I can only guess the identities of the Reflection and the Revenant. But how could I not know who the Destroyer is when my darling Casimer's name means 'Destroyer of Peace'?"

Nils gazed down at her with a smug smile. "You are mistaken, my Queen. The King's name means 'Bringer of Peace.'"

"No. That is the most commonly assigned meaning, but his name is associated with both."

"She is correct," Casimer said. "I didn't expect either one of you to know something so obscure."

"I try to know everything about you, my darling," Echidna said, brushing his cheek with the back of her hand. "I think the first lines bring good news to you. Though we do not know what attempt is being planned, or who is planning it, you will foil it and spill their blood instead."

"I agree with that interpretation," Nils said. "But the second part seems to support my suggestion to send the prince away to the country estate."

Casimer nodded solemnly and placed his hand over his heart. "The dragon's mark sounds like it could refer to the tattoo identifying the Marisianne royal heirs. There is only one living person other than myself with such a mark, and that is Ladon."

Echidna jerked to her feet, no longer able to remain perched on the arm of the throne. "Ladon is just a child. He adores you. He would never harm you."

Casimer regarded her sadly. "You know that I adore him as well. Yet this prophecy is vague, as they always seem to be. It does not include a time frame. The events described here could take place tomorrow or many years from now. And it specifically says the sword will not be wielded in malice. That makes it sound even more likely to be Ladon's doing."

"You said prophecies are nonsense," Echidna protested. Crimson cheeks betrayed her emotion as she struggled to maintain her composure. "With no time frame, how long do you plan to send him away? You would be sending your own son away out of fear of what *may* happen."

"Indeed, I only gave this prophecy consideration based on your advice," Casimer said calmly. "I can't imagine that Ladon would *ever* wish to do me harm, but who is to say these lines don't warn of a tragic accident? My decision is not based on this prophecy alone, however. I was already considering sending him to the country estate to protect him from the sickness. This additional piece of information merely solidifies my decision."

"So you are sending our child away?" Echidna demanded, her eyes stinging with unshed tears.

"Yes, until a cure has been found to this mysterious illness and I can determine the value of this prophecy. You must see that it is the most logical course of action."

Echidna set her jaw and stared up at her husband, wishing she had never uncovered those vile words. Nils stood behind the throne, a ghost of a smile on his lips. She spun around so she didn't have to look at the pair any longer and put one foot in front of the other, marching toward the door before her tears could spill over.

"Echidna, my dearest, we aren't finished yet. Where are you going?" Casimer called out from the throne.

A hot tear leaked out from the corner of her eye, but she resolved not to let him know how upset she was. She took a deep breath, and when she answered her voice rang through the room, steady and strong.

"Where my son goes, so do I."

10

NIGHTMARES OF RABBITS AND WOLVES

Desta

Desta flopped down to the ground and promptly pulled off her shoes to rub her sore feet. She didn't care that she was sitting in dirt. It didn't matter that there was a rock poking into her aching bottom. She was sitting, and that was enough. After traversing a seemingly endless series of switchbacks up the mountainside, the group had *finally* reached the top of the old trade route leading to the bridge that crossed the Ameles River.

Navigating the switchbacks had been maddening. The road was so steep and so eroded from years of neglect that it had been necessary to lead the horses instead of ride them. For every hundred feet they walked, they progressed only thirty up the mountain. It was no wonder that the road had fallen into disuse over the years and been forgotten. Desta wished she could forget it too. No sane person would ever use this road.

Now, as she watched Jarold and Leal survey the bridge, and for the first time since she left home, she had serious misgivings about her decision to come along on this journey.

Not because she missed her mother, even though she did, and not because she was growing homesick, even though she was—a little bit. No, her misgivings sprang directly from the fact that she was certain the bridge was going to crumble away beneath her feet, sending her to meet a premature end at the bottom of the ravine.

The stone arch perched so precariously at the top of the gorge that it looked like an errant breeze could blow it right off. In reality, the bridge was supported from underneath by stacks of sturdy slabs that jutted out from the cliff at an angle, each longer than the one below. The parapets were dotted with the crumbling remains of winged statues, but they were now so worn it was impossible to tell exactly *what* the creatures were originally supposed to be.

"Are you feeling alright, Desta? You look pale," came Caeneus' gentle voice.

Desta pried her eyes away from the bridge and turned her attention instead to where Caeneus and Raysel were tending the horses. She waved one hand in front of her face. "I'm fine! Don't mind me."

However, her protests were not enough to stop Caeneus from handing Alba's reins to Raysel and coming over to check on her. He patted the top of her head soothingly before taking a seat on the ground beside her. "That face you're making seems to indicate otherwise," he said.

Desta forced herself to smile. Caeneus always went out of his way to be kind to her, so the least she could do in return was present an upbeat attitude. "You really didn't need to come over here. I'm just feeling nervous about crossing the bridge. Is that thing really safe enough for us to use?"

Caeneus was quiet for a moment. He watched Jarold and Leal creep closer to the center of the bridge, using long rods to examine the stone and pausing to mark with chalk any problematic areas they found. "We won't take any chances. If it's impassible, then we'll have to go back down and find another way across."

Desta scrunched up her nose in distaste. "I'd rather not do that either."

"Same here," Caeneus agreed with a hearty laugh. "They look to be more than halfway finished now, so I think we'll be able to cross. What I'm worried about is figuring out where we are going to make camp for the night. It took longer than we anticipated to get here. There won't be time to make it to Kisoji before sundown. If the roads were better, we could press on to Kisoji in the dark, but it's too risky with them in such terrible condition."

"It's probably just as well," Desta said. "I'm exhausted. I don't want to take even one step farther than I absolutely have to tonight."

"Me neither," Raysel said as he dropped down beside Caeneus with a groan. He pulled off his shoes as well and then leaned back on his elbows, sighing blissfully as he wiggled his toes. "According to Alden's map, there's a village about a mile away where we can stay for the night."

A clatter arose from nearby, and Desta's brows furrowed in confusion. If there was sudden movement anywhere, she expected it to come from the bridge, but Jarold and Leal continued their methodical inspection uninterrupted, oblivious to the noise. Then the wagon rocked from side to side, and Cole burst out of its back door. The red-faced twin scampered down the steps, howling with laughter the whole time.

Not a second later, Rian appeared in the doorway. He was also red-faced but not from laughter. A thin, squiggly object flew from his hand to hit Cole squarely in the back of the head. "That was not funny!"

"It'sss jussst a little payback for you being the only one who getsss to ride inssstead of walk!" Cole hissed.

Rian responded by whirling around and slamming the door shut. Still laughing, Cole picked up the object, which Desta could now see was a toy snake, and rejoined his brother who was kneeling beside the wagon to check the wheels and undercarriage.

Eloc watched the entire proceedings with a conspiratorial grin on his face. "I told you it was worth stopping by that toy shop in Rhea," he said, giving his brother a congratulatory clap on the back.

"You really shouldn't have done that," Raysel scolded, but he was so tired that there was little emotion behind his words. "You might have caused him to reopen his wounds."

Eloc shrugged. "Rian's tough. He can handle a little prank. Besides, the doctor said he was fine."

"The doctor said he's supposed to avoid strenuous activity for a few more days," Desta corrected. "That's why he is riding instead of walking."

Raysel stood and brushed himself off. "Although I'm sure his injuries are fine, I should probably go check on him."

How strange, Desta thought. She had expected Caeneus to be the one to check on Rian. After his discharge from the hospital, she had seen Caeneus lingering outside his room at the inn several times. Now that she thought about it, she didn't recall ever seeing him actually go in. They had seemed to be getting along better lately, so what had changed? Maybe Caeneus felt guilty that Rian had been injured in the process of retrieving the book from the cave.

Desta glanced up and caught Caeneus watching as Raysel entered the wagon. The wistful look on his face disappeared as soon as he realized she was looking at him.

"I'm sure he doesn't blame you for his injuries," Desta said in an attempt to be comforting.

A look of surprise crossed Caeneus' face, and he gave her a small smile. "I know that, but thank you for saying so. I just don't know what to say to him right now."

Desta was tempted to ask him to elaborate, but Caeneus laid back into the patchy grass and closed his eyes, so she didn't feel right pressing the issue.

Soon after Jarold and Leal finished their inspection, Desta found herself holding Aki's reins and standing behind Caeneus and Alba. The group had formed a single file line in order to avoid putting too much stress on any one area as they crossed. She nervously traced circles in the dirt with her toe while clutching the reins with sweaty hands. Although there were plenty of noises around her, the only sound Desta could hear was the gravel grinding beneath the wheels of the wagon as it slowly, but steadily, lead the way across the bridge. Caeneus signaled for her to follow, and they also began to cross, being careful to avoid the weak areas Jarold and Leal had marked. Seeing the bridge's condition up close did nothing to alleviate Desta's jitters. Every inch of the stone was riddled with hairline cracks and pockmarked with small craters and pits. However, despite her fears, everyone made it across without incident, and the bridge rapidly faded into the distance.

They arrived in the village as the last saffron rays of the sun were sinking into the horizon, painting the houses and shopfronts in the myriad hues and shadows of sunset. The thatched roofs and gingerbread trim on the houses gave them a cozy appearance despite their small size. In another time, this place would have looked like it came from the pages of a storybook—except something must have gone horribly wrong in this story. Desta stared in dismay at the once quaint cottages that were now marred by broken and cracked window panes, missing doors, and sunken roofs. Weed-choked window planters hung askew or lay in pieces on the ground. Several of the buildings had burned down, leaving their sooty skeletons as the sole evidence of their former existence. There was no way to tell if the fires happened before or after the village was abandoned.

"Well, this looks like a *great* place to stay for the night, Raysel," Eloc said, his voice filled with false cheer.

Raysel shot him a sidelong look. "Until we get closer to roads that are on our current-day maps, I can only go by what is shown on this old one from Alden."

Caeneus stepped up beside Raysel. "I suppose we shouldn't be surprised. If this village were inhabited, the roads would have been better maintained and the bridge would still be frequently used."

"That's the kind of sound logic we needed a few hours ago," Cole said, tempering his sarcasm with a wink. "There wouldn't have been any better places to stop anyway."

"There are definitely worse places to sleep," Leal said. He grabbed one of the glow lamps from its hook and then hopped down from the driver's seat of the wagon. "Let's split up and see if any of these buildings are suitable to use for shelter. At least then we won't have to set camp in the open."

Three hours later, Desta gratefully wriggled into her bedroll. Though none of the houses or shops had seemed safe enough to stay in, the twins had found a ramshackle barn that was ideal for their needs. It was large enough to keep the horses and wagon inside with them. Plus, the half-missing roof provided enough circulation that they had been able to light the cook fire on the dirt floor of the building, shielding it from view in case anyone else happened to be nearby.

She rolled onto her back and stared up into the rafters where patches of stars twinkled in the gaps between them. Now that she was warm and comfortable, exhaustion quickly overcame her. Her last thought before she fell asleep was to hope for pleasant dreams.

Desta stood in front of a stone cottage with a peaked roof that was surrounded by a white picket fence. A short distance away from the house was a larger building. Somehow, Desta knew it was a workshop. The scent of fresh ink and paper filled the air, and long green grass swayed gently under a surreally perfect blue sky. The peaceful scene looked like it came straight from the pages of a storybook.

As she watched, the front door swung open, and she realized it was hinged at the top like a pet door rather than on the sides like normal. Six black-and-white rabbits hopped out into the yard. Desta watched in wonder while they cavorted in the sunlight, flipping their ears and wiggling their tails while pulling bright orange carrots from the garden and arranging them in the yard.

First they placed the carrots in neat lines to form a perfect triangle. There was something important about the shape, but in her dreamy state Desta couldn't place the significance. The rabbits paused in their play only long enough to eat the carrots, and she laughed to see them devoured with comical speed. Once every bit had been consumed, green tops and all, they then began pulling a second set from the garden.

This time, they were arranged to form letters and Desta watched with rapt attention as each word became clear. "Help us," she read aloud. It was so peaceful here, and they had been playing without a care in the world, so why did they need help? Were they asking for *her* help?

There was a bright flash of light, and the rabbits fled in a panic, one cotton tail after another disappearing through the door. Desta heard a low, snarling growl from nearby. She turned toward the sound, and three wolves popped into existence, their lips curled back menacingly as they slowly circled her. Instead of having a pair of fangs, each wolf had a single, oversized fang that extended well below its muzzle. The wolves lunged at her in unison, hitting with enough force to send Desta tumbling backward, the air pushed from her lungs as she contacted the ground.

Desta shot upright in her bedroll, gulping desperately for air even though there was nothing to impede her breathing. She glanced around the barn, half expecting wolves to appear, but they didn't. Everything was just as it should be. One of the horses stamped its foot and snorted softly while the remnants of the fire burned low. Cole's silhouette reclined, undisturbed, in the open doorway where he kept the night watch. Beside her, Caeneus stirred in his sleep, muttering something incoherent before rolling away.

"What's wrong?" Raysel whispered.

Desta flinched in surprise and looked to the left to find Raysel propped up on one elbow with his other hand wrapped around Thorn's hilt.

"I had a nightmare about rabbits and wolves," she replied as she slid back under the blankets. "I'm sorry that I woke you."

"Do you want to talk about it?" he offered.

She rubbed her eyes and lifted one of the shutters from the glow lamp sitting on the ground between them. "Thank you, but no. I'm going to make some quick notes and then go back to sleep."

Raysel pulled Thorn back into the bedroll with him and yawned. "Alright, but if you change your mind, you know where to find me." Desta smiled at his little joke, and he gave her a sleepy grin in return.

She pulled her notebook out from beneath her pillow and tugged the pen loose from the spine. The dream had been both vivid and detailed, similar to the one she had on the night the Senka operatives attempted to raid their camp. But that dream had been so realistic that she didn't realize she was asleep until she actually woke up. This one was different. She had known it was a dream the whole time, and it didn't seem to carry any clear message. Still, could the carrot triangle have symbolized that it had some connection to the books the group was seeking? Or was it just a collection of her random thoughts from earlier in the day?

It didn't matter which answer was the right one. Desta recorded the dream in as much detail as she could recall and then shuttered the lamp, but it was a long time before she was finally able to fall back to sleep again.

In her second dream of the night, she found herself in her mother's kitchen. As she sat at the table writing in her notebook, an army of gingerbread men began to pour forth from the oven in a steady stream. They swarmed over her feet, impotently nipping at her toes with their tiny icing mouths.

It was the third dream of the night—in which the gingerbread men returned, this time streaming in from the garden through the pet door and swinging carrots like swords—that led her to write off the visions as mere absurdities created by her imagination rather than meaningful foresights. When she closed her eyes again, she finally drifted off into blissful, dreamless sleep.

11

TURNABOUT

Nerissa

By midmorning the next day, Nerissa and Alba plodded behind the wagon on the road leading to Kisoji. The surrounding foothills were covered in a light fog, which was not so dense that it significantly impaired her vision, but it *was* hazy enough to match Nerissa's mental state. Although it had become a habit to go to bed early and rise with the sun each day, her body would never grow accustomed to doing so. It simply wasn't in her nature. And so, while the others passed the time by trading light banter as they rode, Nerissa remained silent, her drowsy mind lost in her own thoughts.

She had experienced a peculiar feeling of being out of place ever since she set foot in Marise. It was not because the land itself felt foreign. After all, the trees and dirt on one side of a bridge were no different from those on the other, even if they were separated by a line that could only be seen on a map. Her discomfort came from the awareness that these were the lands ruled by Casimer. Never mind that he also controlled her country at the moment—Chiyo was still *her* country no matter who held the throne. Being in Marise had summoned to the forefront of her mind a thought that she had been suppressing for a long time.

She hadn't embarked on this journey with the intent to take control of Marise from Casimer, yet the reality of the situation was becoming harder to deny with every passing day. In the back of her mind, she had always known that it wouldn't be possible to retake Chiyo without first completely removing Casimer from power. He had already proven that he was not the kind of man who could be dealt with through diplomacy. She simply hadn't wanted to acknowledge to herself that when she deposed Casimer, she would take control of all of Renatus by default. It didn't matter how justifiable her motivations were. In the end, she and Casimer would be the same—usurpers who stole a country from its rightful ruler. The thought disgusted her, but it didn't weaken her resolve. Her one choice was to keep moving forward, trusting that the remaining portions of the prophecy would contain a solution to her conundrum. The prophecy's reference to the "lost suspension technique" gave her at least a spark of hope. Once Casimer was neutralized, she could consult with the Chiefs to determine the best approach to transition to power in Marise.

"I can see the village from here!" Desta exclaimed, snapping Nerissa out of her reverie.

The village situated at the bottom of the slope was tiny, perhaps only slightly larger than the one Shae and Desta called home. The stream running along the eastern edge of the settlement was wider than the road that passed through it. Given its size and remote location, it was no wonder that Kisoji was omitted from most maps.

As expected, their entry into the village created quite a

stir. A group of young children discarded their toys and scurried right up to the wagon. Men and women peered out of windows or called out greetings from their workshops.

"Are you traders?" a small boy asked.

He was promptly shoved out of the way by another boy who asked, "More importantly, do you have candy?"

"Chocolate candy!" a little girl repeatedly exclaimed while twirling around in circles.

Nerissa shared a sidelong glance with Raysel. "Those kids are so excited that it might be dangerous to give them candy," she whispered.

"Dangerous to who? Us or their parents?" Raysel replied with an impish gleam in his green eyes.

"Do you suppose traveling candy trucks come this way often?" Desta murmured.

"I don't think there is such a thing," Eloc began.

"But they may be onto a lucrative business idea," Cole said, finishing his brother's sentence.

Jarold leaned down from the front of the wagon to answer the children's excited inquiries. "I'm afraid we don't have any candy to sell, but we do have antiques and books."

"Who would want those?" the first boy lamented as three youthful faces turned crestfallen in unison. Having completely lost interest in the newcomers, the children scurried back to resume their play as if they had never been interrupted.

Leal chuckled while Jarold watched the children run off. "I think I'll have to get some sweets to bring home with me," Jarold said wistfully.

"I'm sure your daughter would love that," Leal said. "Be sure to bring something for your wife too, or you might not have as welcome a homecoming as you expect."

"That's an excellent point," Jarold replied with a laugh.

It was then that Rian stuck his head out from the side window of the wagon. "When is someone going to get around to opening the back door? It's bad enough that I have to be tucked away like a useless lump when we're on the move. Do you plan on keeping me locked in here while we're stopped too?"

Raysel sighed patiently as he dismounted, and he handed Borak's reins over to Nerissa. "We've only been stopped for a short time. And you know you're not actually locked in. The stairs just block the door when they are folded up."

"I may as well be locked in," Rian groused. His eyes met Nerissa's briefly, but she looked away too quickly to see his expression brighten.

It wasn't that she was intentionally avoiding him since their conversation at the hospital in Rhea. Yet there was a part of her that felt relieved that Rian had to spend the greater part of recent days inside the wagon. She still hadn't figured out how to behave around him. Although, deep down, she wanted nothing more than to talk to him, whenever the opportunity arose, she reflexively shied away. It wasn't like her to be intimidated by someone, but the situation she found herself in now was anything but normal.

She felt her cheeks warming and her lips turning upward automatically at the memory of the way he said he would never forget her eyes. Her desire to talk to him was motivated as much by wanting to get to know him better as by the fact that he might be able to fill in some of her missing memories. Ironically, it was the same desire that caused her to distance herself as well. Although she had managed to keep her true identity a secret so far, Rian was too observant for her to feel comfortable letting her guard down around him.

Raysel unfastened the latches holding the stairs in place and had to jump back as Rian sprang from the wagon like a cat from a water basin.

"What should we do first?" he asked eagerly.

"Caeneus and I will talk to the residents to find out if any of Barr's relatives still live here," Raysel answered. He gestured toward a handful of townspeople who were making their way toward them. "Jarold and Leal will stay with the wagon to handle any purchases or trade inquiries. *You* will stay here with the others and help tend the horses."

Rian huffed in frustration. "I'm perfectly capable of coming with the two of you to look for Barr's family."

Raysel reached out and patted Rian's lower back in a seemingly amiable gesture that caused Rian to flinch. "You're also perfectly capable of pouring oats into the horses' feedbags."

Rian's hand drifted automatically toward Bane's hilt, but he turned away without another word. Nerissa was surprised to see a wicked, almost triumphant-looking smirk flicker across Raysel's face. She barely heard him mumble something that sounded like "turnabout" under his breath before he took back Borak's reins.

Though they were strangers, the villagers were initially warm and welcoming to Nerissa and Raysel. None showed any hesitation to chat, and some even invited them in for tea or coffee. However, a consistent trend emerged immediately upon the mention of Barr's name. The talkative miller, who had been reclining on his porch swing on a self-described day off, suddenly remembered a pressing task he had to attend to. The housewife next door to the miller sniffed the air, claiming to smell a burning pie that was apparently beyond sensory perception. The poor potter had been so startled by the mention of Barr's name that his clay had collapsed and spun right off the wheel.

Nerissa's feet dragged in the dirt after the fourth such departure. "Going back to the wagon won't get us anywhere," she whined.

Beside her, Raysel clenched and unclenched his fists in frustration. "Talking to more of the villagers obviously isn't going to help either. I'm afraid, if we upset them too much, they might run us out of town. Then we'd really be at a loss."

Seeing an unexpected movement out of the corner of her eye, Nerissa turned. On the other side of the street, a brawny, weathered-looking farmer was sitting on the back of an unhitched cart laden with a variety of gourds. Having caught her attention, the man waved again.

"Come and see my pumpkins—they're fresh off the vine. I'm sure I have exactly what you're looking for," he beckoned, wiggling his eyebrows significantly as he said the last part.

Nerissa grabbed the back of Raysel's shirt and gave it a tug, but he had already spotted the man and stopped walking as well. He glanced over his shoulder at her and shrugged. "It won't hurt to talk to him especially since he seems willing to talk to us."

"Hopefully, he wants to talk about more than just pumpkins," Nerissa murmured.

The farmer reached behind him as they approached. When he turned back, he was holding one of the most perfectly formed pumpkins Nerissa had ever seen. "Isn't this one a beauty?" he asked, not bothering to hide his pride.

"It's lovely," Nerissa replied awkwardly as he pushed the pumpkin into her arms. "It would seem a shame to eat it."

The farmer frowned and shook his head slowly. "It will go to waste if you don't eat it. The real shame would be in not using it to its fullest. Even the seeds will be delicious if you roast them with spices and a bit of sugar."

"You seem like a practical man," Raysel said. "How much do you want for it?"

The man nodded sagely. "I *am* a practical man. You must seize every opportunity presented to you to make a living as a farmer."

"You have a point," Raysel replied. "How much would it be for two pumpkins and a half dozen squash?"

Nerissa's head turned back and forth between the two men as they talked. She did not understand why Raysel was buying gourds instead of asking what the man knew of Barr's family, especially when her arms were beginning to ache under the weight of the pumpkin.

The farmer nodded, satisfied. "Fifteen gold for the lot. If you make it twenty-five gold, I'll throw in something extra."

Nerissa scowled as the situation became clear. The farmer wasn't trying to sell pumpkins, or rather, that wasn't his sole reason for getting their attention. He wanted to sell information. She seriously questioned the scruples of anyone who would withhold information for money.

Raysel, however, didn't seem phased in the slightest by the man's tactics. "Twenty gold now and five more once I see the quality of your 'goods,' " he said.

"That's fair enough. First, why exactly are you looking for Old Barr?" the farmer asked, smiling shrewdly as Raysel handed over the coins.

"How did you know who we were looking for?" Raysel countered instead of answering.

The farmer pulled off his hat and blotted at the dirt on his cheeks with a cloth. "I could overhear your conversation with the miller from here."

"We were entrusted with delivering to him a modest inheritance from a distant relative," Raysel said. The lie rolled off his tongue so smoothly even Nerissa almost believed it—and she had helped him invent the story. "Their will noted that if Barr had already passed on, the items should be given to his immediate family instead."

"Old Barr never had any family as far as I know, though he does have a housekeeper and her son living up there with him. Or at least he did. There's no telling if he's still alive in that ancient mansion of his or not."

"So his home is not actually in the village?"

The farmer seemed to find the question quite funny. "Oh, no indeed! That grand estate is likely larger than all of this place put together. It was here long before this little village was founded and likely will be here long after too. You'll have no trouble finding it if you follow that path north for a handful of miles." He paused long enough to point to a dirt road that was even more worn than the main one. "You're likely to find quite a bit of overgrowth on the road though since no one ever goes up that way."

"No one comes or goes from the house?" Nerissa asked. "That's somewhat abnormal, isn't it? We noticed your neighbors are reluctant to talk about him. Is that a part of the reason?"

"It's all a load of foolishness, if you ask me," the farmer replied. "The rumors around here say there's something unnatural about both Old Barr *and* his house. They claim he's hundreds of years old and that some magic about his house makes him immortal."

"And you don't believe those rumors?" Raysel prodded, giving no hint of his own opinion on the topic. Considering Alden's great-grandfather's claim that Barr was over 300 years old, Nerissa herself wasn't so willing to dismiss the stories as baseless.

The farmer laughed again. "I've seen Old Barr with my own two eyes, though not in decades. Believe me, no immortal being would be more wrinkles than skin. What person in their right mind would believe in such rubbish? These people have so little excitement in their lives that they have to invent fantasies to have something to talk about. Myself, I have too much work to do to get involved in idle chatter."

Apparently, you still have plenty of time to listen in on all the "idle chatter," Nerissa thought, sharing a glance with Raysel.

"I guess there are advantages and disadvantages to living in a small town," Raysel commented.

"Now that's the truth! My farm is a few miles off in the other direction, and I'm sure there's no shortage of rumors about my kin and me either." The man stood and began gathering squash in his arms. "Do you find the quality of my 'goods' satisfactory?"

"Indeed, I do," Raysel answered. He handed the man a five gold coin and accepted a pumpkin and three of the squash in return.

Though her arms were now thoroughly numb, Nerissa smiled resolutely as the man piled the remaining three squash between the top of the pumpkin and her chin. She could just imagine the looks on their companions' faces when they returned with enough gourds to feed them for a week.

12

OVER THE WALL

Nerissa

Nerissa never would have guessed it was possible, but the road between the village of Kisoji and Barr's estate was in worse condition than any they had previously encountered. In fact, it was so densely riddled with bumps, ruts, and grooves that it was almost a misnomer to call it a road at all. While the conditions weren't particularly problematic for those on horseback, the same could not be said for her three companions driving or riding inside the wagon. Nerissa cringed sympathetically when the wagon dropped into one of the numerous craters and lurched precipitously, sending Leal skidding sideways along the driver's bench into Jarold's shoulder.

No sooner had it righted itself than the side window was thrown open, and Rian's head popped out, his expression fierce enough to send a swarm of angry bees back to its hive. "Can someone *please* explain to me how this is supposed to be better for my health than riding?" he demanded. "This road—if you can call it that at this point—is so bad that even the potholes have potholes. Jarold, Leal, stop the wagon so I can get out!"

His appeal, however, elicited no response from either one of them.

"I don't think they can hear you over the horses," Raysel said.

"Raysel, either let me out *right now*, or I swear I will let myself out by climbing through this window."

"You've nearly recovered from your injuries. I don't think you really want to reopen them by tumbling out of a moving wagon," Raysel said. "If you're really that uncomfortable, I'll ask Jarold to stop so we can saddle Keme for you."

"Uncomfortable?" Rian squawked. "A seesaw would provide a more stable ride!"

Nerissa stifled a giggle but not quickly enough.

"What do you find so funny?" Rian snapped.

Her eyes narrowed, and she arched one brow coolly. "Wait a minute, Raysel. Let's not be hasty. Releasing that beast may not be such a good idea after all. What if his barking frightens the horses?"

Rian's lips pressed into a thin line. Before he could respond, the wagon hit yet another bump, jarring the window loose so that it dropped onto the back of his shoulders. A string of curses instantly poured from his mouth, which was mercifully muffled when he yanked his head back inside and slammed the window shut.

After that, there was no need for Raysel to ask Jarold to stop. Rian's outburst caught his attention, and he brought the wagon to a halt on his own. He twisted around in the driver's seat to cast a quizzical look back at the rest of the group. "What's all the commotion about?"

"Rian wants out," Raysel answered simply.

"I don't blame him. My aching backside wouldn't complain about a short break," Jarold said.

Leal's head bobbed in commiseration. "I could use a break myself. Although I like Jarold, I'm quite tired of sliding into his lap every few minutes. Besides, it would be a good idea to check over the wagon too. I started to hear an odd rattling about a half mile back."

Raysel looked up to where dark clouds were gathering in the western sky. "It looks like it may rain soon, so Caeneus and I will ride ahead while you do that."

"Not without me," came a muffled shout.

"Think it's safe to let him out?" Raysel quipped.

"If we don't, I have a feeling it won't be the road that tears the wagon to pieces," Nerissa said with a wink. "Still, Rian may lose his temper quickly, but he cools down just as fast. I'm sure he'll be back to his usual self by the time we get to the estate."

"Caeneus, Rian, and I will ride ahead while you check the wagon," Raysel amended loudly enough for Rian to hear. "Cole, saddle Keme. We're leaving as soon as Rian is ready."

Alba tossed his head, mirroring the frustration Nerissa felt as she studied the wrought iron gate that blocked them from reaching the manor. Though the ornate filigree of the ironwork was beautiful—and clearly crafted to impress visitors—the estate's atmosphere could not have been less welcoming. Ominous clouds continued to collect overhead, cluttering the sky and covering everything in a gray pall. All of the windows were shuttered. Not a hint of light or life leaked through the slats. Ivy had engulfed the bottom half of the building, giving the appearance that the house rested in a nest of greenery. Though Nerissa couldn't put her finger on it, something about the ivy seemed out of place.

None of those things looked as inhospitable as the stone wall. Standing more than ten feet high and extending as far as the eye could see, it completely encircled the grounds. Even the wall surrounding the Royal Manor hadn't been that tall. Nerissa supposed that the difference arose from the fact that the one around the Royal Manor was intended to serve as a demarcation of the property limits, not prevent intruders. Regardless of how opulent the estate must once have been, *this* wall was clearly intended to keep people out.

The gate and the wall were not the only things about this place making Nerissa uncomfortable, however. She scowled and rubbed her ear for what seemed like the hundredth time, despite knowing that doing so would not rid her of the pervasive humming sound. At first, it had been so faint she couldn't tell if she was really hearing anything at all, but the closer they got to the house, the louder the sound grew.

"Well, if the heat of Caeneus' gaze could melt metal, we would be inside already," Raysel said wryly. "Since that approach doesn't seem to be working, we're going to have to find a different way in. There's bound to be another opening in the wall somewhere."

Rian shifted in Keme's saddle. "Are we sure there's any point in trying? There's no sign that anyone lives here anymore."

"We need to go inside even if the place is empty. We have to find out what the source of this noise is," Nerissa said, rubbing her ear again.

"What noise?" Rian asked.

Raysel and Nerissa turned to him with identical expressions of incredulity.

"The annoying hum," Raysel answered. "It seems to be coming from somewhere near the house."

Nerissa nodded in agreement. "It's distinct enough now that I can hear the pitch rising and falling in a steady rhythm. Can't you hear it too?"

Rian looked baffled. "Are you trying to trick me?"

"You really can't hear it? It sounds like the buzzing of a bee," Raysel said.

"Why can you two hear it and I can't?"

"I'm not sure, but I don't think Caeneus and I are the only ones," Raysel said. He pointed to Borak's ears, which were in constant motion, twitching side to side. Keme's and Alba's were also rapidly flicking around as if the animals were trying to locate the source of the sound.

Rian tilted his head to the side, straining to catch a hint of the sound. "I can't hear anything out of the ordinary."

"I wonder why you can't hear it," Nerissa said. She cast an uneasy look toward the house. "Still, whatever the reason, we can't find the source or the book if we don't go inside." A soft pattering sprang up, and a fat, cold drop of water splattered against the back of her hand.

Rian pulled the hood of his cloak over his head and urged Keme into motion. "Then we will have to find a different way in—and the sooner, the better."

Nerissa pulled up her own hood and pressed her legs into Alba's flank, nudging him to follow Rian and Raysel along the perimeter of the wall. Fortunately, it was not long before their efforts were rewarded. Just out of view from the front of the house was a smaller side gate. The distinct lack of rust on its hinges made it apparent that this entrance was used far more recently—and frequently—than the main one. It swung open easily, emitting a soft squeak in the process.

There was a hitching rail conveniently located beside the gate, so they tied up the horses and set off in the direction of the house. The gate was merely the first piece of evidence that the estate was not as uninhabited as it initially appeared. Inside, there were many more telltale signs. A short distance ahead, a pair of chickens scurried across the gravel path, clucking furiously and leaving a trail of feathers in their wake. All around, the grass was lush and green, neatly trimmed, and free of weeds. Even the ivy growing up the exterior had been carefully cut back to keep the doorway clear. Wispy curls of smoke rose from the nearest chimney into the gloomy autumn sky.

If Nerissa were thinking logically, she would have been elated by the knowledge that the estate was indeed inhabited. Yet something else had captured her attention. Halfway between the house and the gate loomed another walled area. Judging by the canopy of trees rising over the top, it was a garden of some kind.

With every step Nerissa took forward, the humming sound grew louder until it became so intense it ensnared all of her senses. It beckoned, drawing her to it like a moth to a flame. She was barely aware of the gravel shifting and crunching beneath the soles of her feet. The hum rose and fell within her body, pulsing like blood through her veins. She veered off the path, her feet carrying her toward the wall of their own accord.

"It's coming from here," Raysel murmured dreamily, drawing up beside her at the base of the wall.

"The sound is coming from inside there?" Rian asked. "We shouldn't go in without going to the house first."

Raysel ignored Rian and reached out, jiggling the handle of the door to the garden. "It's locked," he said.

Rian grabbed Raysel by the shoulders from behind and shook him. "Did you hear me? What's *wrong* with you? If you want to see what's inside, we should go to the house and ask them to open the door."

"No, I have to get to the source of the sound. I guess we'll have to climb over the wall," Raysel said, unaffected by Rian's attempt to rouse him.

"I was thinking the same thing," Nerissa agreed. She grasped the top of a protruding stone and wedged her toes into a gap, lifting herself from the ground.

"What? No, no, no!" Rian exclaimed. "Why am I suddenly the voice of reason?"

Heedless of Rian's consternation, Nerissa moved her foot to the next gap just in time to elude his lunging grasp. She was carried upward by an all-consuming desire to reach the source of the noise. It was so tantalizingly close now that she could hardly bear the anticipation.

After hoisting herself onto the top of the wall, she grabbed an overhanging limb and shinnied down the tree trunk. Raysel and Rian dropped to the ground beside her seconds later, but her eyes were fixated ahead. Standing in the center of the garden was a ring of six geodes, each nearly as tall as Nerissa, that had been cut in half to expose their crystal-encrusted interiors. They were beautiful, mesmerizing.

Although Nerissa felt Rian's hands pulling at her clothes, she was too busy reveling in the giddy feeling that encompassed her. It flowed out from the pillars like an unseen river, and she longed to touch it. Drowning in it would be bliss. Her hand extended forward, straining toward one of the crystal points which was now only inches beyond her reach. Beside her, Raysel did the same.

Nerissa didn't hear his exclamation of pain. She didn't see him crumple to the ground. Her fingers kissed the cool stone, and a jolt of fire shot through her body. For the briefest moment, she saw a green-eyed woman sitting at the center of the ring where no one had been a moment before. Blackness laced in from the edges of her vision, and a distant part of her knew she was falling. Immediately before consciousness slipped away, she heard a voice cry out her name, and a pair of warm arms enveloped her.

13

ONE LESS OBLIGATION

Nerissa

Nerissa opened her eyes a short time later to find herself in a spacious, but sparsely furnished room. Feeble gray light filtered in through rain-streaked window panes, and a fire crackled in the hearth on the opposite wall. The constant humming in her ears had gone back to being a gentle, distant buzz. Though the privacy curtains hanging between the elaborately carved bedposts obscured most of her surroundings, she could see enough to conclude that this was a room inside the manor. She could also see that she wasn't alone. Raysel stalked back and forth across the foot of the bed, the floorboards creaking with his every step while Rian leaned against one of the posts. That was odd. Normally, Rian would be the one doing the stalking, while Raysel would be the one behaving calmly. It didn't take long for Nerissa to realize why their roles were reversed.

"Keep your voice down. Do you want our conversation to be overheard?" Raysel rasped, his voice tight with restraint. "To answer your question, no, that's not what it was like at all."

Rian huffed in vexation, but he kept his tone low as well. "Well, if you didn't lose control, how else can you explain your behavior? The two of you walked into that trap like lambs to the slaughter! You're supposed to be her guardian. How exactly can you say you were keeping her safe when you weren't even in control of yourself?"

Nerissa snapped her eyes shut as soon as she realized they were talking about her. It wasn't right to eavesdrop, but she was too curious to speak up. There would be no harm in pretending to be asleep for a little while longer.

She heard Raysel sigh heavily, and the creaking of the floorboards slowed. "I'd like to say I don't know what came over me, but I do. I remember every bit of it. The attraction to that place was irresistible. Being near that ring of geodes was absolutely exhilarating."

"It must have been," Rian murmured. "You were so caught up in the moment that nothing I said or did got through to either one of you."

"Are you really sure we were in danger? It's hard to believe. I can't remember the last time I felt this good."

"If you doubt you were in danger, then you're *still* not thinking clearly!" Rian hissed. Nerissa could feel the bedpost shaking from his animated gestures. "Use your eyes! You may have recovered quickly, but Caeneus hasn't awakened."

"I can't explain it," Raysel said softly. "It was unlike anything I've ever experienced before. She must have felt the same thing."

Nerissa silently agreed with him. Weren't you supposed to

be tired or weary after fainting? Like Raysel, she couldn't remember ever being so energized.

"What if there is another place that has the same effect on the two of you? How can you protect her then?" Rian asked.

Rian's accusation must have struck a nerve. The creaking halted, and when Raysel spoke again, his voice was a raging whisper. "What are you insinuating? That I shouldn't be her guardian? That you would be a better choice because you were unaffected? Because if you think that—"

Rian cut him off. "Raysel, don't take that line of thought any further. There is no one more fit to be her guardian than you. You've misunderstood my point. I'm bothered as much by my own inabilities as by yours."

Nerissa had only seen Raysel lose his temper once before, so she couldn't resist the urge to open her eyes a sliver and peek at the pair.

"I know, I know. It still stings, even if you don't mean it to be an insult," Raysel replied, rubbing his face with one hand. Nerissa felt the bedpost shake again as Rian nodded his head. "I'm painfully aware of my inability to resist that place, but what do you mean by *your* inabilities?"

This time, it was Rian who sighed. "While you were being drawn into that place, I couldn't see or hear anything out of the ordinary. How am I supposed to protect her—or you— from something that I can't sense? You have no idea how helpless I felt when you both collapsed. I couldn't do anything but catch her before she fell." His voice cracked as he said the last part.

Nerissa was so astonished by his rare display of emotion

that her eyes flew all the way open. Just as they did, a woman who appeared to be in her early thirties entered the room, pushing the door open without stopping to knock.

"Good, you're both awake," she said when her eyes met Nerissa's.

Rian's and Raysel's heads swung toward the bed. Neither of them said a word, but Nerissa could see that Rian's cheeks were flushed. He was probably wondering how much she had heard.

"I thought you would appreciate some water," the woman announced. She strode across the room to place the tray she carried on the nightstand beside the bed. "Now that you've had ample time to recover, it would be best if the three of you were on your way."

"We couldn't possibly…," Rian began.

"Impose on our hospitality any further?" The woman finished his sentence with a curt smile. Her gaze lingered on Raysel and Rian, who now wore their hair loose and draped down their backs to dry faster. Her eyes shifted toward the fireplace where three swords stood propped against the drying rack that held their cloaks.

"I was trying to say that we couldn't possibly leave without getting answers about what happened in that garden," Rian corrected.

"Answers? What is there to answer? You came onto our property uninvited, and your friends were overcome by the cold and the rain," she replied tersely. "I went against the wishes of the master of this house by giving the three of you shelter temporarily after we found you in the garden. Now you are making me regret that kindness by refusing to leave."

Rian opened his mouth to argue again, but Raysel quieted him by putting a hand on his shoulder. "All we ask is to talk with the master of the house for a few minutes. Rian has already told you that we didn't come here with the intent to trespass. We are with a group of merchants who are searching for antique books. We came here at the recommendation of Governor Alden of Rhea. Surely, the master of the house can spare a few minutes for a group sent by the governor."

The woman pressed her lips together so tightly that they formed a thin, white line. "I will convey your message, but do not be surprised if he refuses to speak with you." The door rattled on its hinges as she pulled it closed behind her.

"Who was she? A housekeeper?" Nerissa asked from the bed. The woman had referred to the master of the house and not to a husband or father, so she must not be a member of the family.

Raysel rushed to her side and grasped her hand so tightly that Nerissa's knuckles cracked. "Oh, sorry," he apologized, immediately relaxing his grip. "I'm so glad you're finally awake."

Rian hovered over Raysel's shoulder. "From what I've seen, there are three people here. That woman, a young boy, and an elderly man. The woman seems to be the elderly man's caretaker."

"Was I unconscious for long?"

"No, you've been out a little less than an hour. I woke up shortly before you," Raysel answered.

Nerissa pushed herself up and scooted to the edge of the

137

bed. "Something about the two of you makes that woman uncomfortable."

"I noticed that as well," Raysel said. "She didn't seem to like the sight of our swords much either. I understand they can make some people feel intimidated, but I don't think that's the case here. It seemed more like she was suspicious of us."

Rian huffed and folded his arms across his chest. "The feeling is mutual. There are a lot of suspicious things going on here. I suppose we should be grateful to her since she and the boy were the ones who invited us in and helped me get both of you into the house. The old man said he didn't care if the trespassers got soaked."

"And why *should* this old man care?" came a gravelly voice. Nerissa looked over to see a hunched, elderly figure supported by a cane in the doorway.

Nerissa climbed out of the bed and bowed along with Rian and Raysel. "Thank you for your hospitality. We apologize for the unusual circumstances of our meeting," she said. "My name is Caeneus, and these are my companions, Rian and Raysel."

"There's no need for introductions. You won't be staying long enough for it to matter," the man said rather than giving his name in return.

Undaunted by his aloof attitude, Nerissa pressed on. "We came here in search of books at the recommendation of Governor Alden of Rhea."

"Yes, yes, so Zada has told me." He pointed at the woman who now stood behind him. "My original question still applies. Why should I care? I do not know Governor Alden."

"No, I wouldn't expect you to know him personally," Nerissa replied, silently reminding herself to remain patient. "Alden's great-grandfather had a close friendship with one of your relatives. Your father or grandfather, perhaps an uncle? His name was Barr."

The man's sagging cheeks puffed out as he harrumphed in response, but he remained silent. With Zada's help, he shuffled toward the room's only chair, taking slow, deliberate steps. He looked so frail that Nerissa would have sworn the creaking sound came from him instead of the floorboards.

"The antique books you are seeking—are you looking for something from a particular author or books in general?" the man asked after easing himself into the red velvet chaise. He propped his cane in front of him and folded his trembling hands over the crook.

Before Nerissa could answer, a young boy loped into the room with a key in his hand. "Barr, I put the box back in the cabinet and locked it as you instructed," he announced. He bounded over and held out the key for the man to take.

"Well done, Matin," Barr said. The words were meant as praise, but there was an underlying thread of displeasure in his tone.

Nerissa mouthed Barr's name, bewildered. There was nothing in what Matin said that should be upsetting unless Barr hadn't wanted to reveal his name. His refusal to introduce himself earlier suddenly took on new significance. Why hide his name if it were simply one he shared with his father or grandfather? Was it really possible that *this* man was the same person who set the trap inside the cave?

"Thank you, son," Zada said. "Why don't you take a few

139

of your toys and go play in the common room?"

Matin scurried across the room and gleefully gathered an armful of handmade toys from a chest beneath the far window. He skipped through the door, pausing only to pick up a small wooden horse he dropped.

Nerissa opened her mouth to ask why Barr didn't want to share his name, but he spoke up first.

"You were about to tell me more about the antique books you are looking for."

It was an obvious attempt to redirect the conversation, but Nerissa was not going to be deterred. She was going to uncover the truth one way or another.

"We're looking for specific books which are part of a six-volume set. We have been able to locate three of them, one of which was in Alden's possession. Perhaps you are familiar with the story, *Barr*?" she said, putting particular emphasis on his name. "Many years ago, you and Alden's great-grandfather tucked it away in a cave for safekeeping."

Zada shifted uncomfortably on the chaise, but Barr laughed. It was more of a wheezy cackle than a joyous sound. "There's no reason for me to answer trespassers' questions. I only came to speak with you because I'm curious to know more about the books you seek. Tell me about the one in the cave. Were you able to successfully retrieve it?"

"Yes, though not without incident," Nerissa replied slowly, trying to puzzle out his reasoning.

"What sort of incident?" Barr asked, thrumming his fingers on the cane's handle.

"We were attacked by a spirit that was protecting the

book."

"All of you?" Barr prompted.

Nerissa's eyes narrowed. She had an idea about why he would ask such a pointed question. "Rian was injured in the process. The spirit attempted to strike me as well, but it was unable to hurt me for some reason." If her guess was correct, Barr knew exactly why the spirit's attacks had passed harmlessly through her.

Barr's fingers stopped moving, and his grip on the cane tightened. "Do you have that book with you? It's been a long time since I've seen it, so I'd like to take a look at it."

"So you *are* the same person who helped hide it and set the trap?"

"I won't answer any of your questions until I see the book for myself."

Nerissa gritted her teeth and looked to Rian for assistance. "It was in the satchel I wore under my cloak. Is that it over there?" She pointed to a cluster of bags hanging from the drying rack in front of the fireplace.

"Yes, the exterior of both of our satchels got wet when I carried you inside, so I put them near the fireplace with our cloaks to dry. Fortunately, none of the dampness got through the oilskin you wrapped around everything," he answered.

"I'm glad I took the extra precaution," Nerissa said as she retrieved the book. She held it out for Barr to examine and waited while he laid his cane aside.

When he finally took it, his hands fumbled along the spine, knocking the pair of crystal fragments from their pocket. Nerissa lunged forward and caught them before they hit the floor. Light radiated out from between her fingers, and one corner of Barr's lips twitched up slyly.

He had knocked them loose on purpose.

Barr stared at the glowing crystals, transfixed. For the first time since they met, he smiled, his cheeks pushing upward, stacking layers of wrinkles beneath his watery eyes. "I'm relieved. This means there is one less obligation I have to burden you and Matin with, Zada."

Zada laid her hand over his. "I am happy you have one less concern, but carrying on your duties is no burden to us."

He lifted his gaze to Nerissa's face. "I've lived a very long time, but I didn't think I would actually live long enough to meet the books' true owner. *Now* I am willing to answer your questions."

14

TALENT

Nerissa

Barr finally pried his eyes away from the glowing stones and turned to Zada. "Please go to my room and fetch the book from the strongbox." She nodded wordlessly and disappeared out the door.

"Does this mean you really do have one of the books we're searching for?" Nerissa asked as Barr handed the book back to her.

He patted the cushion, inviting her to sit beside him. "Yes, I do have one of them, but that fact should not have been known to anyone outside this house. I'm quite curious to learn how Governor Alden knew to send you here as part of your search."

Nerissa perched herself on the edge of the chaise and took a deep breath to collect her thoughts. Her mind reeling from the discovery that the man in front of her was, in fact, the same one who set the trap in the cave so many years ago. That, together with the strangely energetic sensation still surging through her, was almost overwhelming.

Finally, Raysel answered for her. "Just as you have been—wisely—reluctant to answer the questions of 'trespassers,' we are also hesitant to reveal our secrets to you."

Barr's features twisted into a wry smile. "I suppose that's fair. I can certainly understand the need for discretion. However, as you may already have surmised, there's no point in withholding information about the nature of the books from me. I am fully aware of the prophecy and the machine diagrams that have been hidden within their pages."

Nerissa recoiled in shock. "How do you know about that?"

"I'd rather not go into the details. It should be sufficient to say that the knowledge was passed down to me by one of my ancestors. He was among those who originally heard the prophecy and created the books as a way to secretly pass it along to the books' true owner."

That explanation was not at all sufficient in Nerissa's opinion. She assumed Shae, Charis, and Alden all had an ancestor among the group who originally hid the prophecy. Yet none of them were aware the books held any significance beyond being a precious heirloom. Barr's knowledge of arcane topics and the peculiarities surrounding his age made it clear there was far more to the story than he was letting on. But if she pressed him on either subject, he was more likely to send them away than to give answers. Still, she would get to the truth before they left. It was a matter of being patient and looking for the right opportunity.

Since he was unwilling to elaborate on how he knew so much about the prophecy, Nerissa decided to try her luck with a related topic. "Alden's great-grandfather referred to the book's true owner as well. Were you really the one who helped him hide the book in the cave?"

When Barr didn't answer right away, Nerissa added, "A little while ago, when you asked to see the book, you said it had been a long time since you'd seen it. That implies you've actually seen the book before. "

Barr looked around the room with wide, innocent eyes. "Did I say that? It must have been a slip of the tongue. I'm an old man, and sometimes I can't find the right words to express my thoughts."

Raysel folded his arms across his chest. "Don't insult us, or yourself, by pretending to be something you are not. We may have met you less than an hour ago, but it is abundantly clear that your mind is far from feeble."

Barr stared sullenly at Raysel and said nothing.

"At this point, even if you deny it, we already know that you were the one who set the trap to protect the book in the cave. I won't ask how you've lived long enough for that to be possible since I can see it is a topic you don't want to talk about. We've already seen with our own eyes the spirit that was protecting the book. Rian was injured by it, and I nearly was too. It's no secret to us that such a creature exists. What I want to know is how you created it."

Barr squeezed his hands into fists, making them appear even more fragile and boney than before. "The choker you are wearing is made from twinned crystals, so you must have some knowledge of how crystals can interact with and alter the energy that flows through them—whether it is light energy, energy of movement, heat energy, or the energy of the human spirit. You are familiar with that principle, correct?"

He waited for Nerissa to nod and then continued. "Just as heat energy can leave behind a burn mark, or light energy can cause fabrics to fade, the energy from the human spirit can also leave marks on places and things. Everyone is aware of this fact to some extent because our spirit can also leave marks on other people. An act of kindness from a stranger can lift you up, while a word spoken to you in anger can linger and weigh you down. Whether you know it or not, you leave pieces of yourself in everything you touch, every place you go. This is especially true for objects or places that are associated with strong emotions."

Nerissa leaned forward eagerly. Listening to Barr talk was like being with Tao again. He was as knowledgeable about crystals as she was—potentially more so.

"You saw the debris in the main chamber of the cave, so you know about the accident that happened there long ago. When that happened, the people who lost loved ones in the incident came to the cave to mourn and say their final goodbyes. Their strong grief and sorrow left a permanent impression on that place."

Nerissa's throat constricted as the memory of the crippling sadness she felt in the cave came back to her. She remembered hearing the funeral dirge, the woman's sobbing, and the cries of a child before the spirit appeared. How could she forget such a thing when the pain of their loss had resonated with her own?

Barr paused for a moment, letting the information sink in. "The crystals with each of the books glow when you touch them because they are programmed to identify you as the one the prophecy is intended for," he said, seeming to change subjects. "Since the crystals contained information about your identity, I used a fragment of the broken stone from Alden's book to make a twinned crystal combination that was attuned to you. It drew on the energy left behind by the mourners to manifest a tangible form—or spirit, as you called it—that could protect the book from being touched by anyone other than you. To put it simply, the spirit was programmed *not* to harm you."

"Don't you think setting a trap like that was excessive?" Nerissa asked. The mere memory of seeing the spirit was enough to get her heart racing—especially now when she could still feel the strange energy pulsing through her. "It was terrifying."

"The trap would never have triggered if you had been the only one to touch the book," Barr said with a shrug.

"That thing could have killed me!" Rian squawked.

"*Did* it kill you?"

Rian spluttered. "No, but—"

"It cut you, repeatedly but not deeply, until Caeneus took the book from you, correct?"

Rian's shoulders slumped. He couldn't argue because Barr was right. "That's how it happened," he admitted. "Although, I wasn't holding the book—I landed on it."

Barr shrugged again. "Holding, touching, I wasn't able to fine-tune the combination enough to make the distinction."

"We didn't see the twinned crystal you used to create the trap. Should we warn Alden that the spirit could manifest again and present a danger to anyone else who goes into the cave?"

Nerissa asked. She didn't want anyone else to be injured by the spirit in the future.

"There's no need to do that. Now that you've removed the book, there's nothing to trigger the trap."

"That's a relief," Nerissa said. The events of that day continued to play through her mind despite her efforts to push them away. She could almost smell the metallic scent of Rian's blood and feel the desperation of trying in vain to light the torch.

Suddenly, heat flared against her chest, and the gentle fire crackling on the hearth blazed into a white-hot inferno. The logs popped and cracked, sending sparks shooting out into the room.

Rian and Raysel sprang into action, rushing to the fireplace to fling their cloaks and bags out of range and stamp out embers before the carpet began to burn. Barr swore and ducked below the arm of the chaise, shielding his face with his hands.

Too stunned to move, Nerissa clutched the pendant through her shirt. It was hot, just like it had been when she started the fire in the cave. She and Raysel suspected the stone had somehow reacted to her desire to light the torch. Had she accidentally used the crystal *now* as she recalled the events of that day?

She didn't *want* to make the fire go out of control. The instant that the thought came to her, the fire winked out, leaving behind nothing but ashy cylinders that had been logs only a moment before and streaks of soot that stained the stone mantle.

"Caeneus, whatever crystals you're wearing, take them off—now!" Barr commanded, panting. His face was bright red and beaded with sweat, though whether that was from the heat of the fire or anger—or both—Nerissa wasn't sure.

She leaned so far away from him that she nearly fell off the chaise, and her hand flew protectively to her neck, covering the voice-altering choker. If she took it off, her voice would go back to normal and Barr would know she was a woman.

"*Those* crystals are twinned. They can't do anything other than what they were programmed for," Barr barked. "You must be wearing an unaltered one with a fire element."

"I-I-I am," Nerissa stuttered. With trembling hands she tugged the leather cord and pendant out from beneath her shirt. "How did you know?"

Barr held out one hand, beckoning for her to give him the pendant. "How did I know? It should be obvious by now that I know a great many things about crystals. And not all of them are things that I'm willing to share."

Nerissa jerked her hand back before giving him the crystal and clutched it tightly to her chest instead. *He knows how I started the fire*, she realized. Ever since she read the fourth section of the prophecy, she thought the reference to drawing a spark from the Heart of Fire was connected to this crystal. If that was true, she couldn't accept that Barr would not share what he knew with her. "I have things that I'm not willing to share either, and I'm not going to hand over this crystal until you answer some of our questions."

Their eyes met, each unwilling to be the first to look away. Nerissa let the pendant slide from her hand and swung it back and forth on its cord like a pendulum.

Barr licked his lips nervously and then leaned back into the cushions with a heavy sigh. "I already told you that I am aware of the prophecy and the machine diagrams hidden within the pages of the books you seek. Those two topics are the only ones I am willing to talk about. The talent is not related to either of them. Please just give me the crystal."

Nerissa froze, and the pendant gradually came to a stop as well. "Talent? What kind of talent are you talking about?"

Barr scowled, the lines on his face deepening until they cut across his face like canyons of light and shadow. "Like it or not, my family has been entrusted for generations with a duty to protect this house and its secrets. I am not going to cast that aside to satisfy your curiosity. I shouldn't have mentioned the talent. It has nothing to do with either the books or the prophecy."

"If the talent is what made the fire go out of control, then it is very much related to the prophecy," Nerissa said. She opened Alden's book, which still lay in her lap, and peeled back the inner cover to read the first line aloud. "Deep in the caves, the inborn talent of the Reflection will draw a spark from the Heart of Fire that will ultimately return an ancient power to the world."

Barr rubbed his face with one hand and sighed again. "I can't argue with that. If the talent is related to the prophecy, it is my duty to share what I know without reservation."

Nerissa handed the crystal over to him. "Then I will let you hold on to this."

"Don't worry, I'm only taking this for safekeeping. I'll give it back when you leave," Barr said. He folded his hands in his lap, staring down at the pendant as he spoke. "This is a complicated subject, so I am not sure where to begin."

"At the beginning," Rian murmured from his seat on the edge of the bed.

If Barr heard his comment, he gave no indication. "I told you earlier that twinned crystals work by interacting with the natural flow of energy around them. This was once called passive crystal use. But there is a second way to harness the power of crystals. Unlike the phenomena brought about by twinned stones, this second method does not happen spontaneously. It requires the user to have the talent—the ability to *actively* manipulate the flow of energy through crystals. Before the Fall of Civilization, it was a common practice, but King Gared issued a decree banning the active use of crystals. Since then, the talent has almost been forgotten even though it still flows through the blood from one generation to the next."

"That doesn't make sense," Nerissa argued. "Why would King Gared do such a thing? None of the histories I've read mentioned him banning anything other than the books on science and mathematics."

"And what do you suppose was the purpose of the ban on those books?"

Nerissa's eyes widened, and her mouth fell open. "I don't know," she admitted. She was so stunned her tongue felt numb as she said the words. Although she had often scoffed at her parents' stubborn insistence on continuing the ban on those books, she had never stopped to consider why the custom began in the first place. Could they have known the reason and never shared it with her, just as they hadn't told her about the existence of the Ohanzee?

"Honestly, I don't know the exact reason for the ban

either. My ancestor either never knew or never chose to share it," Barr said.

"How could you tell that Caeneus has the talent?" Raysel asked. "How did you know it was him and not Rian or I who made the fire go out of control?"

Barr squinted at Raysel for a moment, straining to see him better and then turned his attention to Rian. "Hmmm. Come closer, Raysel. I want to get a closer look at you," he said instead of answering the question.

When Raysel obliged, Barr took him by the chin and peered at his eyes. "I see. *Both* of you have the talent."

"How can you tell we have the talent?" Nerissa asked.

"The talent is one that you inherit from your parents. It so happens that the ability to use crystals is associated with having green eyes. Though not everyone with green eyes has the talent, everyone with the talent has green eyes. The color tends to be a little bit greener than normal. You both probably have had many people comment on how remarkable your eyes are."

Nerissa understood the concept of inheriting traits from one's parents. It was the same principle that governed various traits when cultivating plants. And she did often receive comments about the color of her eyes. Without thinking, Nerissa glanced at Rian, and her lips curved upward as she remembered him saying he would never forget her eyes.

Her smile drooped when she realized Rian looked thoroughly irritated. "I get it. Raysel and Caeneus are *special*," he said.

Barr shook his head again. "No. The talent may have

been forgotten, but it is not particularly rare."

Raysel stood and took off his crystal pendant. "If you say I have the talent too, I should probably give this to you."

"Ahh, a spirit crystal with an earth phantom. This is a rare gem, indeed," Barr said, cupping the pendant in his palm. "I will hold onto it for now too—just in case."

Nerissa was dying to ask Barr how to actively use crystals, but Zada stepped into the room carrying a thick, leather-bound book with her. The crystal tucked into its spine glimmered in the light from the fire. "I'm sorry I took so long," she said, and then Cole and Eloc's faces appeared on either side of the doorframe behind her. "It seems we have some more visitors."

15

SILENCE

Nerissa

Nerissa sat on the floor in the dining room of Barr's home while a constant drizzle sent silvery ribbons sliding down the window pane in front of her. The cloud-covered sky had just begun to change from the pitch black of night to the dim gray glow that heralded the rising sun. It was far too early in the morning for Nerissa to be awake, but she felt restless and the ever-present humming sound had made it nearly impossible for her to sleep. Though they had not intended to stay here overnight, their unfinished business with Barr was not the only reason why they stayed. The damage caused to the wagon by the deteriorated road was more extensive than anticipated. Jarold and Leal had been able to patch it up well enough to reach the house, but the constant rain prevented them from making the full repair. Barr had reluctantly agreed to allow them to stay overnight, giving them enough time to complete the work. Nerissa was secretly grateful for the excuse to stay longer. There were still numerous questions she needed answers to.

Reflection: Thorn of the White Rose

Despite the draft rolling off the window, she was kept warm by the heavy curtains that draped around her like a cocoon. Warmth wasn't her sole motivation for sitting like this while the others slept, however. It also gave her sufficient illumination to read by without allowing stray light to reach the rest of the room to wake the others prematurely. The book Barr had given her the night before lay open across her lap, and she read over the words for what seemed like the hundredth time.

> The second section of the prophecy is as follows:
>
> The will of the Reflection is the catalyst that guides the fate of the reborn land. They will not seek revenge, but will instead seek to take back the stolen throne. Though the Reflection does not know it, they were born with the power needed to suspend the Destroyer's actions.
>
> All the while, a Traitor toils unnoticed under the Destroyer's command. The Destroyer will be too caught up pursuing his ambitions to recognize the approaching danger, and no guardian's sword will shield him from it. The Traitor will raise the dead, and they will walk, recognized yet unrecognized, amongst the living.

This portion of the prophecy didn't offer any guidance like the third and fourth sections did, but she was sure Casimer would have found the last half to be invaluable. If there were a traitor under her command, she would want to know who they were—either to expose them or to closely monitor their actions. But it didn't really matter to her who Casimer's traitor was unless they were willing to assist her efforts to take back Chiyo. Perhaps they would be.

And then there was the reference to the walking dead. Even though she couldn't fathom how the dead could be brought back to life, at least this passage provided a clue as to who would be responsible for it.

Her eyes scanned the lines of the prophecy again and again, analyzing them for deeper meaning, when a movement in the yard caught her attention. Through the haze of rain, she saw Zada holding an umbrella for Barr as they slowly made their way from the house to the walled garden. Matin dashed ahead of them carrying a small black case and an umbrella of his own.

Now that's interesting, Nerissa thought. *What are they planning to do in there? It must be important enough to venture out into the rain at such an early hour.*

She forced herself to turn her attention back to the book. No matter how intense her curiosity was, she had to respect Barr's need for privacy. He said it was his duty to protect this house and its secrets, and she, of all people, could understand the importance of protecting one's secrets.

Still, Rian couldn't hear the humming sound. After questioning the rest of the group the night before, she had discovered that no one else in their group could hear it either. Since she and Raysel were the only ones who could hear the sound, and they were the only ones with the talent, the most logical conclusion was that there must be a connection between it and the ring of geodes. And if the ring was connected to the talent, it might also be connected to the prophecy.

Her eyes flicked back to the window. The door to the garden hung open, swaying gently in the rain. It would be easy to slip through unseen. The overgrown shrubs and bushes within would provide excellent cover, allowing her to observe the three of them undetected.

Nerissa thrummed her fingers softly along the fore edge of the book. If she went in, would she really be able to resist the draw of the crystal pillars? Even here, inside the house, the humming sound called to her, keeping her from being able to sleep. She told herself she was being foolish and stared down at the prophecy, unseeing.

Several minutes passed, and Nerissa found herself gradually being lulled to sleep by the steady patter of rain on the glass. The only other sound in the room was the soft drone of someone's snoring. Her eyelids grew heavy, and her chin sank to her chest.

It's finally quiet. The thought drifted languidly through her mind, and then her eyes shot open. The *only* other sound in the room was the snoring.

The constant humming was gone.

That was the last straw. It took every ounce of her willpower not to throw open the window and run straight into the garden. Instead, she laid the book aside and carefully extracted herself from the curtains.

"Raysel," she whispered, crawling up beside him to gently nudge his shoulder.

He blinked up at her with bleary eyes, and Nerissa hurriedly pressed one finger to his lips. "Shh! We don't want to wake anyone."

"Is something wrong?"

Nerissa shook her head. "Do you hear it?"

"Hear what?" Raysel rubbed his eyes. "Just tell me what's going on. That incessant humming kept me awake most of the night."

"That's what I'm talking about. Do you hear it or not?"

Raysel threw back the cover of his sleeping bag. "It's gone!"

"Shh!" Nerissa repeated, waving both hands frantically. "If you can't hear it anymore either, then it's not my imagination. I saw Barr, Zada, and Matin go into the garden a few minutes before the sound disappeared. Let's go find out why."

"We shouldn't do that. If we get caught, Barr would be angry—and rightfully so. We need his cooperation."

Nerissa grabbed his hand and tugged, urging him to get up. "The humming sound and the talent have to be related. Aren't you curious about that place? Don't you want to know why we fainted when we touched those pillars? You're used to moving around in the shadows. He'll never even know we're there."

Raysel's lips twitched back and forth as he considered how to respond.

"If you're trying to be quiet, you're doing a terrible job of it," Rian mumbled. He rolled over in his sleeping bag to face them. "Raysel, tell me you're not actually thinking about sneaking into that garden a second time."

Raysel's hesitation answered the question for him.

Rian ran his fingers through his hair, pushing the tangled black strands out of his face. "Get ahold of yourself, Raysel. Between the two of us, you're supposed to be the rational one.

After what happened last time, you should know better than to go back there too, Caeneus."

"The sound stopped—," Nerissa began.

"You don't need to rehash your argument for me. I heard everything you told Raysel."

"You've been awake this whole time?"

Rian shrugged. "I'm a light sleeper. I've heard you rustling around in the curtains for a while. It would be foolhardy for the two of you to go into the garden again."

"And you think letting this opportunity pass by is a better idea?" Nerissa hissed, glancing around to see if anyone else was awake.

"I said it's too risky for the two of you to go in. On the other hand, it would be far less risky for me to go in and report my findings back to you."

"That is a much safer alternative," Raysel admitted.

Nerissa's lips puckered like she had bitten into a lemon. "We don't have time to sit around and debate what to do. If Rian goes in alone, then everything we learn would be second hand. If we aren't going to learn anything useful, there's no point in anybody going in. Rian can be our backup to make sure we don't lose focus. We're all going in together."

Raysel hesitated, but Rian was already tying his hair at the base of his neck in preparation to go. "Fine. Consider yourselves warned though. I'll do anything I have to do to keep you two from touching those pillars again. I'm not going to be gentle."

"Agreed," Nerissa said, and Raysel nodded his

concurrence.

They crept out of the dining room and then hurried down the hallway to the kitchen. A pot of oatmeal simmered on the stove, and a carafe of freshly brewed coffee was kept warm beside it, filling the room with its rich aroma. Barr, Zada, and Matin clearly didn't intend to be gone for long.

After checking to be sure the yard was empty, they dashed out the back door and didn't slow until they were close enough to press their backs against the garden wall.

Raysel shot her a quizzical look. "Now that the sound is gone, I don't feel drawn inside like I did before, do you?"

"No, I don't," Nerissa replied. "There's something else that seems strange too." She glanced around, trying to put a finger on what it was about the exterior of the house that bothered her. When it finally occurred to her, she was ashamed to have overlooked something so obvious—particularly considering her studies in the field of horticulture at the university.

"That's it!" she said. "All of the plants here are strangely green for this late in the autumn. Don't you find it odd? The grass and the ivy growing up the outside of the house should be turning brown by now, and yet all of the plants in this area are as green and lush as they would be in the summer."

"I didn't think much about it," Raysel replied. "They're probably late to change because we're so high up in the mountains."

"No, that's definitely not the reason. If anything, the leaves should change *sooner* here. Elevation profoundly affects when leaves turn for the season."

"Enough chatting. Now is our chance," Rian said. He peered into the open doorway of the garden. "I can see them from here. They're doing something near the circle of geodes, but they have their backs to us." He slipped through the door, crossed the gravel walkway, and ducked into a row of overgrown hedges in a matter of three bounding strides. Raysel and Nerissa followed quickly behind.

Once safely inside the hedges, they dropped onto hands and knees and crawled forward, ducking beneath branches and staying close to the ground.

Rian swatted at a spot on his neck with a stifled curse. "Why do hedges always have to be full of bugs?" he murmured.

"Do you crawl through shrubbery often?" Nerissa asked in a hushed tone.

"No," Rian whispered, but there was a lilt in his voice that made it sound more like a yes. "Keep it down. We're close enough to hear them talking now."

Nerissa stretched out in the dirt, wriggling as close to the edge of the greenery as she dared in order to get a better view.

On the other side of the branches, Barr stared down at an object in his hand. Zada stood nearby, pressing a cluster of spirit crystals against the side of one of the tall geodes. "That's enough for this one, Zada. Matin, are you ready to move on to the next point?" he called out.

"Yes, sir," the boy chirped from the opposite side of the circle.

"Now, you tell me what we are supposed to do next," Barr said in a tone Nerissa recognized well. It was the same one Tao used during lessons.

"I'm supposed to move on to the next pillar, working in a clockwise motion. Then we count down from five so that mother and I touch the crystals to the pillars at the same time," the boy answered.

"Very good," Barr praised. "And why is it important that the crystals touch at the same time?"

"So that the energy flowing between the two pillars remains synchronized," the boy recited.

"Correct," Barr said, and he began to count down. When he reached the end, Zada pressed the cluster of crystals against the pillar in front of her and held it there, just as she had done before.

"I'm surprised you allowed them to stay overnight," Zada said, turning to look back at Barr over her shoulder as she spoke. Her face was hidden so deeply in the depths of her cloak that only the tip of her nose was visible.

Barr tapped the end of his cane on the ground. "Although I would prefer for them to leave as soon as possible, part of my duty is to help Caeneus fulfill the prophecy. I don't know exactly what it says, but I do know fulfilling it is necessary for the good of Renatus in the long term—and that is worth any amount of short-term discomfort. Still, it's dangerous for them to get close to this place, and it has nothing to do with the prophecy. I want to be rid of them before they have a chance to snoop around this garden again."

Too late for that, Nerissa thought.

"I know that I will be relieved when they leave. Even though they wear their hair differently, my heart nearly burst from my chest when I first saw their long hair and swords. When I left my husband, I was convinced that he was too caught up in his pursuit of power to bother looking for us, but the sight of those men shook my confidence. I thought the Senka had discovered our hiding place after all these years."

Nerissa's ears immediately perked up at Zada's mention of the Senka. She heard Rian inhale sharply, and there was a soft crackling on either side of her as both he and Raysel eased forward.

Barr shuffled over to Zada and laid one hand on her arm. "You are safe here. You left Nils twenty years ago when Matin was an infant. If he were going to send a search party for you, he would have done it long before now. And, even if he did send some of his men to seek you out, they would be looking for a middle-aged woman and a twenty-year-old man, not a young woman and her five-year-old son."

Nerissa snapped her mouth shut, afraid a bug would fly in if she left it hanging open for long. Matin was supposed to be twenty years old? That meant they were the same age. First Barr seemed to be unnaturally old, and now Zada and Matin were older than they appeared too. A line from the fourth section of the prophecy echoed in her mind. Could this be the place where time stands still?

Nerissa couldn't see Zada's expression, but when she spoke again, there was less tension in her voice. "I remember those days like they were yesterday. By the time I got here, I was out of money and almost out of food. Those 'friendly' villagers didn't look kindly on a young woman traveling alone with a child. I assume they suspected some sort of scandal." She stopped and laughed scornfully. "I visited each house looking for work until someone finally suggested I check here.

Looking back on it, it must have been their idea of a joke, but I didn't know any better at the time. All I cared about was finding a place remote enough that we would be out of the Senka's reach in case Nils did come looking for us. It was the hand of fate that guided me here, and I am as grateful as ever that you were willing to take us in."

Barr looked away and coughed awkwardly into his fist. "Don't get overly sentimental on me. You know this is a mutually beneficial arrangement. After my wife and son took ill, there was no one left to carry on my work. Now you and Matin will inherit the care of this estate."

Barr turned slightly, just far enough for Nerissa to see that he was holding another, smaller cluster of twinned crystals. Five points protruded from its center, and two of them were glowing. As she watched, a third one flickered with light and then went dark again. It seemed to be a measuring device of some sort. Barr looked down at the device and frowned.

"Something is wrong," he said.

Alarm filled Zada's voice. "Something's wrong with the shield? The prisoner isn't going to escape from the suspension, is she?"

Suspension? That's the second time I've come across that word recently—and it's not a commonly used term, Nerissa thought. There was no time now to dwell on the significance though.

"Unfortunately, I don't have any way to check the integrity of the suspension directly," Barr answered calmly. He turned his attention to Matin. "Matin, how are things going for you?"

"My fourth point is lit up. It's nearly done," the boy

replied, hidden from sight by the pillar.

"Is this one of the geodes they touched yesterday?" Zada asked, alarm rising in her voice.

"No, and there were no irregularities when we reset the shield yesterday." Barr's brow furrowed. "If Matin's pillar is behaving normally, there must be something near here that is drawing energy away."

"Another crystal? Maybe Raysel or Caeneus dropped one when they fainted."

Barr looked toward the entrance where the door hung open. Then his eyes shifted, raking over the dense foliage within the garden. "It could be another crystal, but more likely it's being caused by some*one* rather than some*thing*. This shield is attuned to those with the talent, so their abilities can interfere with it even when they aren't actively attempting to manipulate the flow of energy."

"But you said as long as they stayed outside the garden wall, it should be safe."

"Yes. That holds true as long as our well-meaning trespassers *stay* out." He lifted his cane and began using it to probe the bushes nearest him.

"Move it," Rian hissed.

"Watch out," Raysel said, but he was too late. Rian was already on his hands and knees crawling away when Barr's cane poked through the leaves. It connected with the tender part of his back, and he couldn't hold back a painful exclamation.

"I knew it!" Barr called out triumphantly from the other side of the greenery. "I don't care which one of you I found, just get out of the garden—now!"

165

A grumbling Rian crawled out first, followed shortly after by Nerissa and Raysel.

"All three of you?" Barr barked. "How long have you been here?"

"Long enough," Nerissa said, keeping her answer deliberately vague.

"I do not appreciate being spied on." Barr lifted his cane again, jabbing in toward Nerissa's chest with each word.

Nerissa grabbed the end of Barr's cane and gently pushed it away. "It isn't our preferred method to gather information either," she said. "But it might be a good thing that we did."

Barr harrumphed. "We'll see about that. Wait for me outside the garden. I'll be out when our task is finished."

16

SUSPENSION

Nerissa

Nerissa huddled against the garden wall between Raysel and Rian in silence, watching faint puffs of breath gather in front of her in the chilly air. Now that she was no longer shielded from the steady drizzle by the canopy of leaves, the rain slowly seeped into her clothes, soaking her to the skin. Why hadn't she thought to grab her cloak before leaving the dining room? She sighed, resigning herself to the dampness. There was no point in dwelling on it now. Regret wouldn't keep her dry.

"Did you hear what that woman said? She's one of the Senka," Rian hissed even though no one was around to hear them.

"She *used* to be one of the Senka," Raysel countered. "She's been hiding from them for twenty years."

"Still, don't you think we could get valuable information from her?"

Raysel shook his head. "I think we're already pressing the limits of Barr's cooperation. He's as protective of Zada as she is of him. If we start prying into her past, he's likely to send us away without answering the rest of our questions. I'd rather we focus on learning more about those crystal pillars than attempt to glean twenty-year-old information from a Senka defector."

His teeth clicked together abruptly as the humming sound returned. The sound resonated in Nerissa's ears, seeming even louder after the brief period of silence. She balled her hands into fists to focus on ignoring its pull.

Rian took one look at their faces and said, "The sound is back, isn't it?"

Nerissa responded with a tense nod, and Raysel muttered yes through clenched teeth. After that, Rian watched the two of them warily, as if he were afraid they would start climbing over the wall at any moment. If Barr kept them waiting too long, Nerissa feared she just might.

A few minutes later, Zada emerged from the garden, casting a scornful look at the trio over her shoulder as she passed. Matin, who followed closely on his mother's heels, echoed her sentiments in his own childish way by wrinkling his nose and sticking out his tongue. Nerissa studied his retreating form with a renewed feeling of astonishment. He might be twenty years old, but there was no indication of it in his behavior or appearance.

Barr locked the gate and then stormed over to the three of them with more pent up fury than a storm cloud, despite his reliance on his cane. "Do you have any idea of the trouble you could have caused?" He stomped one foot in frustration and answered his own question without giving them a chance to respond. "No, that's a foolish question—of course you don't. Let me rephrase that. *Why* did you follow us into the garden after we explicitly told you to stay away?"

Nerissa lifted her chin and chose her words carefully. She wasn't going to apologize, but she didn't want to say anything that would further provoke his ire. "We followed you because we believe that ring of geodes is related to the prophecy. I will show you the passage that proves it."

The rain picked up in intensity, pelting Barr's umbrella before rolling off the back in streaming beads. "I very much doubt that, but I will give you the opportunity to explain." He turned his back to them and shambled along the gravel path toward the house. "First go dry yourselves off. Those books didn't survive the passage of hundreds of years just to have you drip on them and smear their ink."

When they returned to the kitchen, Barr was already waiting for them at the table. Nerissa was glad he had chosen to have their discussion here since it was the warmest room in the house. Although she had changed out of her wet clothes, the dampness still clung to her hair and shoes. She took a seat beside Barr while Rian and Raysel brought out the books and placed them on the table, ready to be used as evidence.

Barr remained silent, eyeing the three of them irritably as Zada placed a bowl of oatmeal in front of him. She took bowls for Matin and herself and left the room without offering any to the others.

Nerissa took Barr's silence as a sign she should be the one to begin. "I would be lying if I said curiosity played no part in our motivation to follow you, but it wasn't the primary reason. Raysel and I both hear a humming sound coming from the ring of geodes in the garden. That was what lured us there in the first place. You said yourself that we both have the talent. We are also the only two people who can hear the humming. Based on those two facts, we surmised that our ability to hear the sound is connected to the talent. Since we already established that the talent is related to the prophecy, it seemed logical to conclude that the source of the sound is likewise related to the prophecy."

Barr harrumphed as he stirred his oatmeal. "That is a rather flimsy justification, in my opinion."

"Perhaps this will convince you," Nerissa said. Rian opened Alden's book and pushed it across the table to her. If her theory was right, this line of the prophecy explained the mysteries surrounding this house *and* the people living in it.

She read the line out loud. " 'They will journey through the ruins in the mountains to the place where time stands still.' The crystal pillars in the garden make time stand still, don't they? We overheard you talking with Zada, so we know Matin was an infant when the two of them came here twenty years ago. How is it possible for Zada and Matin to age no more than a handful of years when they have lived here for twenty?" She rushed on without giving Barr an opportunity to answer. "We have also heard rumors from several sources that you are over three hundred years old. I never gave the tales any credence until this morning, but after hearing your conversation, I now know otherwise."

Barr continued stirring his oatmeal in silence, and for a moment, Nerissa was afraid he would refuse to answer. Then he said, "Yes, the ring of geodes does make time stand still, though you've reached the correct conclusion for the wrong reasons. There is a discrepancy between our physical and chronological ages because the pillars slow the passage of time for everything within the immediate area. As soon as you stepped within the outer wall at the perimeter of the property, the three of you began to age more slowly too."

"How is that possible?" Nerissa asked.

"The crystal pillars you touched in the garden alter the flow of time, making it flow at one-fourth its normal speed. The effect radiates outward, influencing everything—and everyone—in the surrounding area."

"So that's why the leaves haven't changed," Nerissa concluded, and Barr nodded in confirmation.

"We've been here for almost a day," she said. "Does that mean four days have passed elsewhere?"

"No, the ring only affects a limited area. The sun still rises and sets here every twenty-four hours."

"You are truly fortunate to have lived such a long life," Raysel said, speaking up for the first time since entering the kitchen.

Barr laughed, though it sounded more like a harsh wheeze. "I'll admit, I thoroughly enjoyed being young and spry four times longer than normal. But I am paying for that now by being gray and achy four times longer than normal as well. I am lucky to have Zada and Matin with me. I began to have difficulties caring for myself long ago."

Nerissa's head tilted to the side thoughtfully. "Earlier, you said you knew about the prophecy and the machine diagrams because one of your ancestors was a member of the group that created the books. Were *you* actually the one who was a member of the group?"

The creases on Barr's forehead deepened, and he snorted. "Those books date from the time of King Gared, more than six hundred years ago. I told you that I'm four hundred years old. You should be intelligent enough to do the math before asking such a silly question."

Nerissa bristled at the insult. Though she longed to voice her displeasure, she knew doing so would be counterproductive. Instead, she swallowed her feelings and pressed her lips together into a thin smile, telling herself that he didn't mean to be as insulting as he sounded.

Rian opened his mouth to respond in disbelief, but Raysel elbowed him in the side so that a soft "oof" was the only sound that came out.

Barr continued, oblivious—or indifferent—to her discontent. "My father, my grandfather, and all of my ancestors spent most of their lives on this estate so they also led unnaturally long lives. It was my grandfather who was a member of the group that created the books. In fact, he was the engineer who made the machine diagrams and programmed the crystals to glow in response to your touch."

Nerissa stared silently at Barr as his explanation soaked in. "If your grandfather created the diagrams, did he teach you what he knew about the machine? Would you be able to start rebuilding it?"

"I'm afraid not, on both accounts. While we have enough food and supplies to be self-sustaining, we don't have access to the materials needed to fabricate the parts. Even if we *did* have the materials, a certain amount of physical dexterity is necessary to assemble the machine." Barr held out one trembling hand to emphasize his point.

Nerissa knew she shouldn't feel so disheartened by the fact that he was unable to recreate the machine. Right now, finding the remaining books was her top priority.

"There's still something that's bothering me," Raysel said, changing the subject. "The prophecy says this is the place where time stands still, not where it slows down. It's a subtle difference but potentially a significant one."

Barr pointed a shaky finger at the next line of the prophecy. "You already heard us talking about it, so there's no reason to hide the answer from you at this point. The explanation is in the very next sentence. 'Here, the lost suspension technique is still remembered.' "

Raysel pushed a stray lock of hair behind his ear. "And how exactly is that related to the pillars?"

"Nowadays, when someone is guilty of committing the vilest of crimes, the punishment administered is death," Barr said, his expression turning solemn. "Before the Fall of Civilization, capital punishment was considered barbaric— even if it was deserved—so the criminal was 'suspended' instead. Inside the ring, where the prisoner is held, the flow of time truly does stand still. The slowing of time outside the ring is merely a side effect."

A thought occurred to Nerissa. "Are there other rings of geodes like this one? If their shields aren't being maintained, can the prisoners escape?" She shuddered at the thought of such criminals walking free among her people. Could *they* be the walking dead the prophecy referred to?

The chair creaked as Barr leaned back wearily. "I have no doubt many others were imprisoned in this fashion. People in the past were no more or less likely to commit crimes than

173

they are today. But there are no other rings of geodes, and there is no risk of those prisoners escaping. At least, not as far as I know."

"Why is this prison different?" Raysel asked.

"A permanent suspension is created when six with the talent manipulate the flow of energy through six identical spirit crystals. The flow of time becomes distorted in the area around the prisoner. When this woman was suspended, an incident occurred, and one of the six involved was unable to complete the process, resulting in the prison being imperfectly sealed. The geodes were put in place to stabilize and reinforce the flawed flow of energy, while the shield protects them from being interfered with by others—accidentally or otherwise."

"And that is why it is so important for Raysel and me to stay out of the garden—to avoid accidentally interfering with the energy maintaining the seal on the prison," Nerissa said.

"Yes," Barr said. "Maintaining the seal on that prison has been my family's duty since before the Fall of Civilization."

"I am sorry our behavior put your duty at risk. If you had explained all of this to us upfront, we would not have gone into the garden a second time."

Barr rubbed his forehead and sighed heavily. "One of the greatest triumphs of humanity is that not a single day passes by without the volume of our knowledge as a whole increasing. It is the reason why we have been able to survive and adapt, even after cataclysmic changes like the Fall of Civilization. And yet, with every passing day, some piece of ancient wisdom is forgotten. The truth about that ring of geodes is one piece of knowledge that *should* be forgotten. I did not wish to pass it on to anyone aside from Zada and Matin. I have shared it with you because you will need the information to fulfill the prophecy."

Nerissa's eyes fell onto the book open in front of her. "According to the prophecy, I can use the talent to suspend Casimer. Since creating a suspension requires six with the talent, it seems I will need to find four others to help me."

"While it's true that six with the talent are required to create a permanent suspension, only two are needed to establish a temporary one."

"Can you teach me how to create a suspension?"

"I can teach you to actively use crystals as well as a horse can teach a fish to swim," Barr scoffed. "I know little of the talent beyond how to identify those who have it. I was taught the theory by which the suspensions are created, but I do not know *how* to create them. All I know is when six with the talent manipulate the flow of energy through six identical spirit crystals, a permanent suspension is created. Two with the talent and six matching crystals are needed to create a temporary one. That is the extent of my knowledge."

"I guess it would be too convenient for you to have all the answers I need."

Barr gave her a wry smile and finally took a bite of his oatmeal. "Whether you were aware of it at the time or not, you have used crystals before. All you must do now is figure out how to use them on purpose."

17

THE WHOLE TRUTH

Charis

Charis had no idea why she cast a surreptitious glance over her shoulder before she pushed open the door to Amon's bedroom. No one else was home. No one had been home for hours, and no one *would* be home for hours. Knowing that still didn't alleviate her nervousness. It had taken her two weeks to work up sufficient courage to do this. She knew it wasn't right to snoop. If nothing else, it was a violation of Amon's privacy. However, after overhearing his clandestine meeting with Casimer's messenger in the library, she felt her actions were justified.

The only reason why she hadn't immediately reported the meeting to her father was the lingering question she had about the notes she had seen the night of the Arts Festival. Amon's translation errors had been subtle enough that they *could* be explained as simple misinterpretations of the context, but Charis doubted that was the case. If Amon habitually made those kinds of errors in his thesis work, her father would have noticed. Since he frequently praised Amon's work, the mistakes must have been made in the research he was doing for Casimer.

A part of her wanted to believe he was mistranslating the documents on purpose. But, whenever her thoughts started down that path, she told herself that she was being naive. Why would he want to sabotage the work he was doing for his uncle?

After taking a deep breath, Charis squared her shoulders and stepped purposefully out of the doorway and into the room. It was now or never. She strode straight to the desk, surveying the room as she went. The bed was perfectly made without a single wrinkle. Not a speck of dust was visible on the dresser or nightstand.

The desk, which faced the wall, was identical to the one in her own room, with three deep drawers on either side of a central pencil drawer. The desktop was as tidy as the rest of the room—and as sparsely decorated. Aside from a single stack of books, a pen and inkwell, and a silver letter opener, the only other item was a framed portrait of an older woman who Charis assumed was Amon's mother.

She opened a drawer and shuffled through the folders within, careful to keep them in order. Each one contained notes on a separate painting, and all of them fit with his thesis work for her father. Charis returned the folders to the drawer and moved on to the next. The second set of files was more of the same. Continuing from one drawer to the next, she grew more frustrated with her inability to find something incriminating. There was nothing out of the ordinary at all.

Her shoulders slumped, and she sank into the desk chair. Perhaps she had been foolish to think that Amon would leave any clues in his desk. There had been nothing to stop her from entering his room in the first place. None of the desk drawers had locks. He was obviously a meticulous person. Someone like that wouldn't leave evidence of his work for Casimer in the open. Then again, a truly meticulous person wouldn't have made those basic translation errors.

Disappointed, she leaned forward, resting her chin in her hands as she stared glumly at the desk. Then it occurred to her. All six of the drawers were the same size, and all of them had appeared to be full. But there had been significantly fewer folders in one compared to the others. So why had it appeared to be as full as the rest?

Charis jumped up so fast that the chair rolled backward several feet before bumping into the side of the bed. She opened the middle drawer and removed the folders, setting them on top of the desk. One look confirmed it—the interior was indeed shallower than the others.

"Ah ha!" Charis cheered triumphantly to the empty room. "This one has a false bottom."

There was no visible evidence of the false bottom in the front part of the drawer, so she pulled it all the way open. There, at the very back, was a thin gap in the seam about an inch long. She grabbed the letter opener from the desk, wedged it into the crack, and pried the bottom up. The wood lifted away to reveal the leather folder she had seen Amon holding at the library. As she picked up the folder, she felt a warm tickle on the back of her neck. She ignored it and began to unwrap the cord, but the feeling came again, this time accompanied by the distinct rushing sound of heavy breathing.

Her own breath caught in her throat. The letter opener

slipped from her fingers and clattered to the floor. She whirled around to see Amon, his arms rigid at his side, his hands balled into white-knuckled fists. Somehow, the stony look he wore was even more frightening than any angry outburst would have been.

"What are you doing?" he asked through clenched teeth.

Charis shoved her hand into her pocket and felt the handkerchief she always carried with her—the one he had given her months ago. She fumbled to formulate an excuse—any excuse—to explain her presence here. There really was no way to wiggle out of this situation. She had been caught, drawer open, folder in hand. But she had to say *something*.

Trembling, she shoved the square of cloth toward him. "I wanted to return this to you. I've kept it for so long that I was too embarrassed to give it back in person. The fabric is expensive, so I didn't feel right keeping it. I was just going to leave it on your desk." It was the best reasoning she could come up with in a pinch, and it was at least partially true.

For the briefest of moments, Charis thought the ruse might actually work. Amon's eyes fell to the handkerchief, and his expression softened. But that look passed all too quickly and was rapidly replaced with rage. With a face like a thundercloud, Amon slapped the handkerchief from her trembling palm and tore the folder from her grasp.

"Did you really think you could use that to get out of this situation?" he hissed. He slammed his free hand down on the desk, looming over Charis as he shook the folder mere inches from her nose. "What did you plan to do with this? How did you even know to look for it?"

Charis opened and closed her mouth over and over like a

freshly caught fish, but she was so stunned that she couldn't make a sound. Finally, her voice tight and quavering, she managed to say, "I saw you meeting with King Casimer's messenger at the library two weeks ago."

Though it didn't seem possible, the look on Amon's face grew even stormier. "Did you tell anyone?"

"N-n-no," Charis stammered.

"Good," Amon said, but his expression didn't relax. "But if you know enough to look for this, then you know too much."

A feeling of dread welled up in Charis' chest at the implied threat in his statement. She ducked away from him and tried to make a run for the door, but she barely made it two steps before he snagged her by the waist, pulling her tight against him. Charis wriggled and clawed at his arms to no avail.

"I can't let you leave now," he murmured in her ear.

Strands of coppery hair clung to Charis' face and covered her eyes, clinging to the wet trails that streamed down her cheeks as she continued her futile thrashing.

"Stop struggling!" Amon shouted as his vise-like grip on her tightened. "You can't tell anyone what you saw! If you do, your life, my life, and the lives of many others will be in danger."

"My life is in danger right *now*." Charis shrieked the words so loudly her ears rang afterward.

"You're right. Your life is in danger now but not from me. I can't let you go until I'm sure you won't do something rash that gets you, or someone else, killed."

There was a pained undertone in his voice that didn't seem to be related to the physical pain she was inflicting on him. The primal part of her mind screamed that she was making a grave mistake, but she decided to trust him anyway.

Amon sighed with relief when she stopped struggling, but he did not loosen his hold. "You can't tell anyone about what you saw," he repeated.

"First you're going to tell me why your research notes are filled with mistranslations. Are you doing it on purpose?"

She couldn't see Amon, but she felt his whole body shudder. "How do you know about *that*?"

"I saw the notes you left on the table in the Special Collection Room on the night of the Arts Festival," Charis answered, realizing too late that she shouldn't have admitted to that so readily.

"The night of the Arts Festival," Amon said slowly, and Charis could almost hear the connection being made as he spoke. "*You* were the one who messed up my bookmarks."

Having no desire to dig herself in any deeper than she already was, she said nothing.

The silence wore on for what seemed like an eternity before Amon sighed again. "I'm going to let go of you now, and you're going to sit on the bed and listen."

Charis nodded and took an unsteady breath as she staggered to the bed.

"You're right," Amon began. "I am mistranslating portions of the information intentionally."

"Why would you do that? King Casimer is your uncle."

Amon laughed bitterly. "You still don't understand? I'm not working *for* my uncle. I'm working *against* him."

"Why?" Charis asked, bewildered.

"He's a murderer," Amon said coldly.

"You began studying with my father long before Casimer's attack on Nerissa's family."

"Do you think the assassination of the Royal Family was the first time he had people killed? When I was a child, he had my father murdered. I suspect there have been numerous others as well."

"He murdered his own brother?" Charis gasped.

Amon shook his head vigorously. "No, my mother is Casimer's sister. My father was a conservative who favored funding the arts over the sciences. He and Casimer publically clashed numerous times as a result of their differing opinions."

"If their feud was so public, how could King Casimer get away with having him killed without anyone suspecting his involvement?"

Amon's sarcastic smile didn't reach his eyes. "It was a tragic accident, of course. A group of nobles, including Casimer and my father, went hunting on a foggy morning. The official story is that my father got separated and was lost in the fog when he was accidentally shot by one of the party members."

"That sounds reasonable enough. Everyone knows it's not safe to go hunting when it's foggy," Charis said.

"It does, on the surface," Amon agreed. "But it's what happened later that reveals the truth. A servant counted the arrows before and after the outing. It's standard practice so they can maintain the inventory of supplies. Although the group reported that one arrow was shot, there were two arrows missing.

Charis started to speak, but Amon silenced her with one finger.

"I know that isn't enough evidence by itself. There's more. Afterward, the examining doctor noted that my father's injury was more consistent with a knife wound than one from an arrow. The doctor was paid a considerable sum to reconsider his report. He didn't get a chance to enjoy his windfall though. He, and the servant who noticed the discrepancy in the number of arrows, mysteriously disappeared shortly after the incident."

Charis inhaled sharply. "How did you learn all of this? You said your father was killed when you were a child, so there's no way you were the one who did all of this investigating."

Amon's answer was evasive. "I told you my life wasn't the only one at stake. That's because I am not working against Casimer alone." He rubbed his arms while he spoke, and Charis could see that his skin was crisscrossed with red marks. She almost felt bad for causing them now.

"So you intended to sabotage Casimer's work from the outset?" Charis asked.

"Yes. I followed in my father's footsteps by studying the arts, so my uncle enlisted my help to research a series of old paintings. He believes they may hold clues to a powerful weapon that King Gared had ordered to be destroyed. Even though it's probably nothing more than a legend, the weapon intrigued him enough to look into it. So far, I have seen no evidence that the tales about the paintings are true. But, if there is even an ounce of truth to them, I want to ensure that the weapon doesn't fall into his hands. Do you now understand why my work has to remain a secret? The man I met with at the library is with the Senka, Casimer's undercover police. If my betrayal were discovered, they would not hesitate to get rid of me like they got rid of my father."

"That explains the similarity," Charis mused without realizing she had actually spoken the words out loud.

"The similarity?"

Charis faltered. She had been thinking of the similarities in appearance between the man Amon met with at the library and Nerissa's protectors, the Ohanzee. Even if Amon were working against Casimer, she still had to keep the truth about Nerissa's survival a secret. "Ah, I mean, it makes sense Casimer would have a group of spies working for him."

"That's not what you meant."

"Yes, it is," Charis said sullenly. "Don't try to put words in my mouth."

"No, it isn't," he insisted, studying her like a hawk studies its prey. "What do you know…" His voice trailed off without finishing the thought.

Charis knew she was a terrible liar. She folded her arms over her chest and focused on remaining silent and expressionless.

"You and Heiress Nerissa were best friends since childhood, and you visited the Royal Manor frequently."

She twitched involuntarily when he said Nerissa's name,

and Amon smirked triumphantly.

"The Royal Family of Chiyo must have a group like the Senka too. You were around her enough that you must have met one of them at some point," he concluded.

While his assertion was not accurate, it was close enough to the truth to make Charis shift uncomfortably.

Amon's smirk broadened into a knowing grin. "Who did you give the book to?"

"What book are you talking about?" Charis bluffed.

Amon gave her an exasperated look. "After everything I've shared with you, you're playing coy with me? You know exactly what book I'm talking about—the heirloom book that belonged to your mother."

"I'm not being coy. I told you the truth at the time. A friend needed to borrow it for their research."

"Alright then, which of your friends was it? What is the nature of their research? Who is their advisor?" He fired the barrage of questions at her one after another.

Charis raised her chin defiantly. If she told him about the books, it might be enough to alleviate his suspicion and keep him from prying deeper. "You shared one of your secrets, so I'll share one of mine. You've already figured it out anyway. A member of Chiyo's 'undercover police' came to me in search of books with crystals in their spines, so I gave it to him."

"Do you know why they were looking for them?"

"No," Charis lied. That wasn't the reaction she had expected him to have. "I just know they were searching for books matching that description."

"We can assume it is part of a plan they have to take back Chiyo."

"I think that's a safe assumption," Charis agreed.

"Then we share a common enemy. I think I might be able to help with their search. Do you know how to get in touch with them?"

"No. They are constantly on the move, so I don't have any way to contact them."

Amon sat down beside her on the bed. "I've been trying to tell you that I'm not as bad of a person as you make me out to be. I can't always tell you the whole truth, but can you at least trust me enough to believe that we're working for the same side?"

Charis laid her hand on his red-streaked arm and said, "Even though you aren't telling me everything, I will trust you." *After all*, she thought to herself, *I'm not telling you the whole truth either.*

18

THE ARROW

Nerissa

Evening sunlight glinted off the crimson crystal cradled in Nerissa's palm, making the fracture lines within shine like hundreds of tiny mirrors. She passed the stone back to Raysel with a tired sigh and shifted to a more comfortable position on her bedroll. It had now been a week since the group left Barr and the village of Kisoji behind. With no specific guidance to follow regarding the whereabouts of either of the two remaining books, they had decided to wind southward out of the mountains toward the more heavily populated areas of Marise.

Since the Senka were aware of their guise as merchants, they could no longer openly enter villages without risking being sighted by Senka informants. That also meant they had to restrict their travel to lesser-used roads and to camp out every night rather than stay at an inn. Fortunately, the twins' costuming skills allowed them to continue their search for the books undercover. Instead of venturing into towns as a group to inquire about antique books, Cole and Eloc donned

187

disguises to scout for family crests with triangles in the design. Although she had seen the twins' skills at work many times, their ability to take on completely different—and convincing—appearances still amazed her.

Today, their travels brought them near one such town, and the group had struck camp early despite having several hours of daylight to spare. Ever since the twins had set off an hour ago, Nerissa and Raysel had been sitting on their bedrolls and trying, unsuccessfully, to use her fire-fire pendant to light a pile of kindling. Neither of them had been able to evoke so much as a spark from the stone. It was the same result they had gotten every night for the last week.

Still, Nerissa knew Barr was right. She *had* actively used crystals before—even if she hadn't been aware of what she was doing. In retrospect, lighting the torch in the cave wasn't really the first time she had interacted with one. So many small oddities from recent months now made sense. It explained why the stone had flashed briefly at Raysel's touch and the warmth she had felt from it outside Darci's workshop.

It also explained her rapid and extraordinary recovery a few days after Ildiko placed healing crystals around her bed despite weeks of little progress. Suddenly, there seemed to be an underlying logic to the unpredictable nature of crystal healing. If she didn't have the talent, would she *ever* have regained consciousness? It wasn't a possibility she wanted to think about.

The rhythmic click-clack of wooden practice swords reached her ears, and she turned to see the others starting their nightly sparring practice on the far side of the camp. Desta sat beneath a tree not far from them, scribbling in the notebook propped against her knees. Nerissa watched as the three men took turns facing off against each other, but her attention was focused on Rian.

In the days immediately after Rian revealed he recognized her, she had been uncertain how to behave around him, afraid she would do something that would give away her true identity. It wasn't that she didn't trust him. She knew he would be as reliable and trustworthy an ally as Raysel.

No, she'd been unsure how to behave because that conversation had made her realize—after all that had happened, and after all the time that had passed—her ploy to attend the masquerade anonymously had ended up giving her something she wanted, something she'd hardly dared hope for before. Too often her heart had been broken by the discovery that an admirer initiated a relationship because of what an association with her could do for him. But now, as long as Rian didn't know her real name, she knew he admired her for who she was and not the title she possessed.

"We've been at this for days, and nothing is working," Raysel said, loosening his grip on the crystal. He had been concentrating so hard and for so long that faint lines remained on his forehead after his expression relaxed.

"I know. Putting in that much effort without getting any meaningful result is frustrating, but giving up isn't an option," Nerissa said, sounding more optimistic than she felt. "If there is any hope at all to use the suspension technique on Casimer, you and I have to master the ability to use crystals at will."

"Mastering the ability to use crystals is not the only problem we have," Raysel said, rubbing his face wearily. "We need to get our hands on six identical spirit crystals too. We could have used the stones from each of the books, but we're missing Shae's, and Alden's is broken in half."

"I've been thinking about that. I used to have a set of wind chimes that were made from seven spirit crystals. No two stones are perfectly identical, but I think you'd find few that are better matched."

"I remember those. While they would be ideal, I don't think there's any chance of finding them in the debris of the manor. Even if they survived undamaged, Casimer's men would have taken anything of value months ago."

"And what if I told you that I know exactly where they are?"

"I'm listening."

"Charis has them. She dug them out of the rubble shortly after the attack. They're hanging in her bedroom window, so all we have to do is ask her for them."

"That's a stroke of luck. Once we have all the books, we can send the twins to Niamh to retrieve them."

Nerissa sat up and held out her hand. "Then all we can do for the time being is focus on figuring out how to use this crystal."

Raysel dropped the pendant into Nerissa's outstretched palm. "If it could be accomplished by concentrating hard enough, we would already have set this whole camp on fire."

"I wasn't trying to do anything when I accidentally made the fire flare up with Barr, so maybe the problem isn't a lack of focus."

"All I know is that I'm taking a break." Raysel then closed his eyes and flopped back onto his bedroll in half-feigned exhaustion.

Nerissa rolled the stone back and forth, watching the reflections of light dance with each movement. At this rate, she and Raysel would go mad from frustration before they made any progress at all. She needed to relax, to clear her mind of all stray thoughts. She needed to push away the pressure to succeed, to think without thinking. *That*, at least, was something she knew how to do. It was an old habit, one that had been driven into her through years of Einar's rigorous training. It was the same habit that had led her to victory in numerous archery tournaments.

She closed her eyes and envisioned herself standing in front of an archery target with her bow in hand, nocked arrow pulled back so that the fletchings brushed behind her ear. Then the image in her mind altered, almost on its own. The archery target became the pile of kindling, and the bow became the fire-fire crystal. All that existed was the target. She reached out with her mind, visualizing an arrow flying effortlessly through the air to strike its center. When the image was firmly embedded in her mind's eye, her fingers released the imaginary string as naturally as they would a real one.

Heat flared from the crystal in her palm, and her eyes flew open in shock. Thin curls of smoke began to rise from the growing flames within the pile of kindling.

"I did it!" she cheered, staring down at her hand in disbelief. Despite the searing heat from the stone, her skin was completely unharmed.

"You did it? You did it!" Raysel said, scrabbling over on hands and knees, his green eyes practically glowing with amazement. "*How?*"

"I didn't really mean to do it, actually. I was trying to clear my mind using the visualization technique Einar taught me for archery, and I ended up changing my focus from the bow and target to the crystal and the wood."

"I was taught a similar technique for sword training, maybe that method will work for me too." Raysel stomped out the flames and gathered another handful of sticks. "Can I try?"

Nerissa reluctantly relinquished the stone. She was eager to try again, but she couldn't deny her friend when he shared her enthusiasm. Raysel sat down and closed his eyes, putting one hand on Thorn's hilt while grasping the crystal in the other. For a moment, nothing happened. Another minute stretched by and still nothing happened. Then, just as Nerissa began to worry the technique might not work for him, Raysel gasped and dropped the pendant. A tiny red-orange flame crawled up the pile of kindling.

"That's hot!" he exclaimed, checking his skin. "How strange. It felt hot enough to burn me, but there's no mark."

Nerissa grinned. "The same thing happened to me too. It didn't burn me in the cave either, even though my wraps were scorched, remember? I think the stones don't hurt the person using them."

"That seems to be the case," Raysel agreed. He pushed back a loose lock of hair with one shaky hand. "I have an idea about why the visualization technique works."

"I'm listening," Nerissa said, repeating Raysel's words with a wry smile.

He grinned back at her, still pleased with his success. "When I was concentrating before today, I only thought of my desire to start a fire and the crystal, and nothing ever happened. Just now, I tried to use the same visualization technique that I do for sword forms, but nothing happened then either. So I decided instead to imagine the bow and target like you did—and that's when it worked."

Nerissa bit her bottom lip as she considered this new piece of information. "That is an interesting observation. So what is your theory?"

"In my initial attempts, there were only two components—the crystal and the wood or the sword and the target. Your visualization technique, however, has three components—the kindling as the target, the crystal as the bow, and the *arrow*."

Nerissa nodded vigorously as understanding dawned on her. "Barr said crystals work when energy passes through them. Maybe that's not so different from how an arrow passes through a bow. We were so caught up focusing on what we can see and touch that we forgot about what we *can't*."

"Exactly," Raysel said. "The talent gives us the ability to manipulate the flow of energy through crystals, so when you imagined the arrow, you unknowingly added the component we had been missing." He closed his fingers over the pendant and grinned as the flame in the pile of kindling steadily grew to be a foot tall, spreading until all of the sticks were on fire.

"No hogging the stone!" Nerissa teased. "I want to try it again too."

"If you're going to start cooking dinner, shouldn't you light the kindling a little closer to the cook fire?" Desta said, strolling up from behind them with her notebook pressed against her chest.

"This isn't for the cook fire," Raysel answered. "We were practicing using the stone."

Desta's eyes widened, and the notebook tumbled from her hands, forgotten in her excitement. She grabbed Raysel's hands, bouncing up and down with glee. "You finally figured out how to use it? The two of you have been working so diligently every night! Your hard work has finally paid off!"

Raysel laughed at her exuberance. "I think you might be even happier than we are, though I'm not sure if that's possible."

Nerissa picked up Desta's pen, which had bounced loose when the notebook hit the ground. As she reached for the book, intending to close it and lay the pen on top, the pages fanned over, stirred by the gentle breeze. They came to a stop on the very last page where the printer's mark was stamped in blue ink. Nerissa jerked her hand back in shock. What she saw was almost as surprising as the heat she had felt from the crystal.

The printer's mark was the outline of a rabbit sitting up on its back feet, gazing at a star. Below, as was done for all modern works, both the city and year of printing were identified. The design itself wasn't what caught Nerissa's attention—it was the way the star was drawn. Instead of being a solid shape, it was drawn to show that each of the five points was formed by a triangle.

Raysel shook his hands free of Desta's grip and came over to Nerissa, placing his hands on her shoulders. "What's wrong?"

Nerissa pointed to the star. "Desta, of all the notebooks you could have chosen from that stationary shop, you picked this one. You really do have uncanny luck."

Raysel squeezed her shoulders, and she could sense his elation. "We will replot our course tonight and set out for the city of Warren first thing in the morning."

19

MY PHOENIX

Nerissa

Hours later, after copious amounts of stew had been eaten, Nerissa sat on the back steps of the wagon with an unopened book on her lap. A cold, steady wind carried clouds across the night sky, making the night darker than usual by allowing only intermittent glimpses of the moon to peek through. Everyone else had already crawled into their bedrolls in preparation for an early start in the morning, but she was too worked up from the excitement of their two breakthroughs to sleep.

Moonlight streamed through a gap in the clouds just in time for Nerissa to catch a sign of movement in the corner of her vision. Momentarily startled, she reminded herself that Cole had the first watch of the night. She saw him sit down at the foot of a tree on the opposite side of camp. When the moon disappeared once again, his form became indistinguishable from the other shadows.

Deciding she was too antsy to read, she slipped the book

back into a trunk and dropped the hand-held glow lamp she had borrowed from Raysel into her pocket. She went to the far side of the wagon so that she wouldn't disturb the rest of the group and drew Harbinger. So much time had been spent focusing on the crystals that several days had passed since she practiced with the sword. Perhaps going over the sword forms would help burn off some pent-up energy.

She had just lost herself in the familiar series of movements when she heard footsteps rustling in the grass and the rattling of a sheathed sword. A cold bead of sweat rolled down the back of her neck, chilled by the autumn air, and she told herself to be calm. Whoever it was, they were probably part of the group. Cole would have sounded the alarm if he had seen an intruder…unless he had been incapacitated. Nerissa shook her head to be rid of the thought. Surely, no one who was this noisy would have been able to catch him off guard. Still, she prepared herself to yell for help and leap into action.

Then a form rounded the side of the wagon, and she heard Rian's voice. "I hope I didn't startle you. I know you're jumpy about sudden sounds, so I tried to make sure you would hear me coming. I take it you can't sleep either?"

Nerissa let out a breath and lowered Harbinger. "No. I know I'm going to be tired in the morning, but I'm not ready to go to sleep yet."

"Do you mind a little company? I didn't get to practice my drawing technique earlier. If you'd rather not have me around, I can go somewhere else."

"No, don't go," Nerissa said, a bit more hastily than she had intended. She tried to play it off by adding, "There's plenty of room here, and since we're out of sight of the rest of the group, there's less chance of waking someone."

Rian nodded, and Nerissa was both relieved and disappointed when he said nothing more. He picked a spot a short distance away and got into a ready stance. In the blink of an eye, Bane was free of its sheath and smoothly arcing out to cut an imaginary foe. The only sound was Rian's foot planting down in the grass and the hiss of air flowing around the blade. He sheathed Bane and started over, drawing the blade free and striking in one continuous motion.

Nerissa knew that Raysel was the First Swordsman of the Ohanzee, but she could see why he and Rian were rivals. Rian may not be able to match his skills in a fight, but she had never seen anyone—not even Raysel—draw their sword that fast.

She turned her attention back to her own exercises with renewed vigor. It would take years to catch up to his skill level, so there was no point in comparing herself to the others. Mastery came through time and practice. For now, her goal was to be able to fight and defend herself well enough that she wouldn't be a burden during a confrontation with the Senka.

Nerissa didn't know how long they continued practicing side by side. Eventually, when her breath was labored and her arms and legs felt heavy, she sheathed Harbinger and sat down in the dewy grass. She heard the click of Bane being returned to its sheath, and then Rian sat down beside her.

They stared up at the rolling clouds in comfortable silence for a time. *Has it really been only a month and a half since we first sat together watching the sky?* Nerissa wondered. So much had happened that it seemed much longer.

"It's a good thing there's not a meteor shower tonight,"

she said, still thinking of the first time they stargazed together. "There are so many clouds that we wouldn't have been able to see it."

"Actually, there will be another one in a few days." Rian's fingers grazed hers as he laid Bane in the grass between them. "We should watch it together, if we can."

Nerissa tilted her head to the side and offered him a tired smile. "I would like that."

"Why do you practice your sword-drawing technique so often? None of the others do," she asked after a moment of silence.

He didn't answer right away, and Nerissa worried the question had offended him somehow. But then she felt his fingers brush hers again, and this time, he didn't pull away. Instead, he laced them through hers and squeezed them gently. Her pulse quickened, and she squeezed back, afraid he would let go if she didn't respond right away.

"When we visited Shae and Desta's village, Shae shared one of her visions with me. It was a warning." His fingers curled even more tightly around hers. "She said my father would attack a woman that I care deeply about and that her life will depend on how fast I draw my sword."

"And that's why you practice so much," Nerissa concluded.

"I would do anything to protect the people I care about. I practice at every opportunity because if the time to act comes and I fail, I would never stop blaming myself. I would always wonder if I could have done more. I already experienced that feeling once, after meeting you and then losing you at the masquerade, and I don't ever want to feel that way again."

Nerissa's throat suddenly felt dry, and her heart felt like it missed a beat. Did he mean what she thought he said, or was she just hearing what she wished to hear?

He leaned toward her, and a ray of moonlight fell on his face, highlighting the intensity of his deep blue eyes. Nerissa's eyes closed in anticipation.

But then he spoke, and her heart sank as he asked the last question she wanted to hear.

"Won't you please tell me your real name?"

"Why is that so important to you?" she croaked and leaped to her feet. She had to leave. If she stayed, she might confess everything to him. She wanted to tell him who she was, and yet she also didn't want to. Indecision twisted her insides, and she yanked her hand free from his.

Before she could leave, Rian was on his feet, impulsively pulling her back and wrapping his arm around her waist. The sensation was pleasantly familiar, though she did not know why. Had he held her like this before when they met at the masquerade?

"Don't go," he said in a husky whisper. He traced her cheek with his free hand and cupped her chin, lifting it toward him. "I want to know your real name because I can't think of you as 'Caeneus' when I think of you like *this*."

In the next moment, her awareness was consumed by the cool breeze through her hair and the soft warmth of his lips pressed against hers. It wasn't Nerissa's first kiss, but it was the first kiss that would remain indelibly written on her heart, holding within it the promise of many more to come.

"Never mind," he murmured when they parted. His arm briefly lingered around her waist before he let go. "If keeping it a secret is that important to you, I don't need to know your real name. I will call you My Phoenix. You were dressed as one the day we met, and like a phoenix, you returned to me when I thought you were gone forever."

Nerissa smiled and put her hands on his shoulders, lifting her heels off the ground to give him a grateful kiss on the cheek. "I think I might like that name even better than my real one."

20

RABBITS AND WOLVES

Nerissa

The scent of ink and paper reached Nerissa's nose at almost the same time that the printer's home came into view. Set at the end of its own lane on the outskirts of Warren, the stone cottage with a peaked roof and white picket fence would have been indistinguishable from numerous other houses in the town if not for the larger stone building—a workshop—standing a short distance behind it.

A cart trundled down the lane going the opposite direction, and the driver lifted one hand casually. Nerissa couldn't see if Jarold waved back, but she was sure he returned the greeting. Based on observations from Cole and Eloc's scouting efforts this morning, the lane leading to the printer's house was frequently trafficked by wagons delivering printing supplies and carts picking up finished books for distribution. So, although they had been avoiding towns and villages until now, the presence of unfamiliar faces on this road would be utterly unremarkable.

Nerissa stood up in Alba's stirrups to readjust her position in the saddle. A bone-deep ache had settled into her legs after riding from sunrise to sunset for three days in order to arrive in Warren as soon as possible. Now that they were so tantalizingly close to the next book, the aching feeling seemed to have been replaced by anticipation. Beside her, Raysel also stood in the stirrups and craned his neck to get a better view of the house.

When they turned into the driveway, Rian rode up from behind, and his eyes briefly locked with hers. She reached up to coyly tuck a non-existent lock of hair behind her ear and immediately felt foolish as her fingers found nothing but air. Why had she done that? Her hair had been short for months. Even if she managed to forget that fact temporarily, she was reminded of it every time someone called her Caeneus. Yet one look from Rian was enough to bring out an old habit.

The corner of Rian's mouth twitched with amusement before he addressed Raysel. "We need to make a small change of plans. Cole and Eloc want to stay with the wagon and have Jarold and Leal accompany us instead."

"We're still going directly to the workshop instead of the house, right?" Raysel asked. "All of the pickups and deliveries are made at the workshop, so it will be less conspicuous to park there."

"Yes. Cole thinks his horse might have picked up a rock in its shoe, so he wants to check it while we go inside."

"That's fine," Raysel replied. Rian nodded and then rode up to the front of the wagon to relay the change to Jarold.

A short time later, having left Desta and the twins to care for the horses, the rest of the group gathered on the workshop's porch. Raysel knocked on the door, but no one answered. They could hear footsteps and voices from within—clearly there were people at work inside. He knocked again and then once more. Finally, a harried-looking man opened the door.

"Pick-ups and deliveries are made around back," the man said. He started to close the door, but Raysel caught it.

"We're not here for a pick-up or delivery," he said. "We are antique merchants in search of books with crystals embedded in their spines. Do you have any matching that description? If not among those in your printing inventory, perhaps you have one in your personal collection?"

A look of surprise flitted across the man's face. He pulled out a pocket watch and flipped it open to check the time. As he did so, he twisted his wrist at an awkward angle, and the gold cover caught in the light, producing a bright flash that left a blue afterimage in Nerissa's vision.

"We are running late for a very important delivery, but I suppose I can spare a few moments for you," he said, fiddling with the watch before putting it away. "I believe a few of our oldest master copies may have crystals with them. Please come inside, and I'll show you where we keep them."

Nerissa raised an eyebrow. Producing copies of the tomes was their business' source of income, and yet the man didn't seem to have reservations about parting with them. Even if the old texts were no longer used for printing copies, they would be valuable. Wasn't he curious about why they were seeking such unusual books? An uneasy feeling tugged at the back of her mind as she followed the others inside.

As soon as Nerissa saw the work area, it was readily

apparent that this was a family-operated business. All of the presses were run by teens with assistance from their younger siblings. They raised and lowered the platens in such consistent rhythm that the sound produced was nearly musical. Type case cabinets stood in the center of the room, their tops partitioned into a grid of compartments containing the metal type used to assemble blocks of text. A teenage girl moved her fingers around the grid with amazing speed, plucking out tiny letters and then deftly planting them into the block of text cupped in her hand. Her two front teeth protruded over her bottom lip as she concentrated, and her eyes never left the book propped open in front of her. Another girl, who was no more than five or six years old, hurried past the group carrying a finished block of text to the presses. At the sight of Nerissa's group, she tripped over feet too large for her petite frame and bobbled the block as she struggled to maintain her balance.

The man's arms shot out, and he bent to steady her with the practiced hands of a parent. "Be careful, Alice. It takes less time to be cautious while walking than it does to gather the letters from the floor and reassemble the block."

"Yes, I understand, Papa," Alice answered. She stood on tiptoes to whisper, rather loudly, into her father's ear. "Besides, Beatrix will get angry with me if I spill her letters again."

The man patted her head tenderly and sent her on her way, but he rubbed his forehead wearily and muttered, "Again?" under his breath once she was out of earshot.

"The master copies are kept over here," he said, turning back to the group. He led them around the outside of the room to the rows of bookcases that stood on the far side.

Nerissa marveled at the size of the collection—it easily

took up half of the workshop's space. She was sure there were libraries with smaller selections of books.

They had reached the first set of shelves when a piercing scream came from outside. The printer reacted by herding his children out the rear door of the workshop. Nerissa watched them flee and wondered if she and the others should follow. Then she caught sight of Cole through the window, ushering Desta into the driver's seat of the wagon while Eloc squared off against a pony-tailed swordsman.

The realization of the man's identity washed over her in a cold wave. *Senka!*

The horses stomped their feet and tossed their heads, eyes rolling wildly in spite of Cole's efforts to calm them. The man swung his sword at Eloc, who dodged by taking several steps backward, drawing the fight away from the wagon. He swung again, arcing the blade in an overhead strike.

Eloc sidestepped to avoid the blow and bounded forward, driving the base of his palm into the man's nose. In one continuous movement, his hand dropped to seize the sword's hilt, and then he pivoted, tucking his shoulder into his opponent's torso. The man flipped over Eloc's back and tumbled to the ground empty handed. Eloc raised the sword above his stunned opponent, and Nerissa tore her eyes away before the final moment of the mortal scene played out.

Just then, the front door to the workshop burst open, and two men rushed inside, swords drawn. Dread of confronting actual Senka swordsmen crept like pinpricks across Nerissa's skin, yet the sensation mixed with relief as she realized they outnumbered their enemies. She drew Harbinger and stepped forward to join Jarold, Leal, and Rian in the skirmish, but

Raysel's arm shot out, blocking her from going past him.

"Get behind me. We will serve as backup," he said, his voice barely audible over the ringing of blades. "No arguments. Too many allies can be as dangerous as too many enemies when fighting in a confined space."

Nerissa knew better than to protest, so she focused on the clashing swords, prepared to jump in if needed. Her shoulders tensed with anxiety as Jarold barely deflected his opponent's strike and was forced up against the type case cabinet. When the Senka man raised his sword again, Jarold feinted to one side and then rolled to the other. The blade connected with the cabinet instead of his flesh, sending a rain of tiny letters throughout the room.

Rian charged to Jarold's aid, using Bane to block the man's next slash. Their blades met over and over in a rapid series of blows. In one final exchange, their swords locked, grinding downward along the length until they caught on each other's hand guard. The Senka man roared wordlessly, thrusting his arms forward with all of his might to send Rian staggering into the first row of books.

The wooden bookcase shook under Rian's weight and creaked ominously, listing sideways before letting go and tipping. It smashed into the bookcase behind it with a splintering thud, knocking over one unit after another like a series of dominos and spilling mounds of books and loose papers into the aisles.

The second Senka man momentarily turned his attention away from Leal to make a lunging strike at Rian while he was defenseless. It was a foolish decision, a desperate bid to even the numbers, and one that cost him dearly. A crimson line erupted as Leal slashed the man's hamstring and sent him sprawling to the floor. His sword skidded away, coming harmlessly to a stop beneath a printing press. Unarmed and unable to drag himself away, the man rolled onto his back. He faced Leal with a look of utter loathing and hurled at him a string of colorful curses which were swiftly silenced.

In the midst of the chaos, Nerissa heard a tremulous cry followed by muffled sobbing. She glanced down the row of shelves nearest her, and there, cowering in the narrow gap between the fallen bookcases with her leg pinched by a fallen shelf, was a young girl. She held the floppy ends of her cloth headband in front of her eyes with one hand and covered her mouth with the other. Tracks were visible on her cheeks where tears had partially washed away smudges of ink.

Nerissa turned back to the fight to see that Rian had recovered and was teaming up against the first Senka swordsman with Jarold and Leal. They had the man cornered, forcing him to defend with both his sword and sheath. It was only a matter of time until one of their strikes broke through.

She tugged the tail of Raysel's shirt. "One of the children is still here, and it looks like she's hurt. I'm going down this row to help her."

"Go on. I will cover you," he said without taking his eyes off the fighters. "But be ready to get out fast if reinforcements show up. We can't afford for you to become trapped. Your life is more important than hers."

"I beg to differ," Nerissa said as she dropped to her hands and knees. She gingerly crawled across the scattered books, mentally apologizing for every torn page and cracked spine.

"Stay away from me," the girl blubbered between hiccupping sobs. "You're one of the bad guys Papa warned us about."

Anger constricted Nerissa's throat. If the printer warned his children ahead of time, then—somehow—he had known they would come. He and the Senka must have been watching and waiting for their arrival. Regardless, no matter how angry Nerissa felt, this young girl had nothing to do with her father's actions.

"I'm not a bad guy," Nerissa said gently. "I'm going to help get this shelf off your leg. Is that something a bad guy would do?"

"No," the girl answered, wiping her nose on her sleeve.

Nerissa struggled to quickly come up with an encouraging response. "You're a tough little girl. Did you know that?"

"My brothers say I'm a baby because I cry a lot." The girl punctuated her argument with a sniffle. "I'm not tough. I want my mama."

Sometimes I do too, Nerissa thought. She didn't remember seeing a woman in the shop earlier, so her mother must have been in the house. "Why don't you tell me about your mama? That way I can take you to her once I get you out of here."

"My mama is beautiful. She brushes my hair every day and ties it up just like hers. And she bakes me gingerbread men cookies. Those are my favorite." The little girl rambled on while Nerissa pushed aside the fallen books and lifted the heavy shelf off her leg. A bright red welt was visible across her shin, but the injury didn't look too serious.

There came a flurry of sword clashes and then a

sickening, guttural sound. Nerissa's chest tightened with fear that it had come from one of her companions. She glanced over her shoulder at Raysel. Although he still held Thorn, she could see the tension melt from his face and knew it meant the last of the Senka had been defeated.

He looked down the aisle, and their eyes met. "It's safe now. If any reinforcements were coming, I can't imagine why they wouldn't have done so by now."

"Does your leg hurt too much to crawl or walk?" Nerissa asked the girl.

She shook her head. "I *am* tough! I'll be ok."

They clambered to the end of the aisle, and Raysel helped each of them stand. He hurriedly slipped his hand over the girl's eyes and guided her away from the fallen Senka. "You don't need to see any of that unpleasantness," he said gently.

"If this was supposed to be an ambush, they were fools to send only two men," Jarold said gruffly. He wiped his blade clean and slipped it into its sheath.

"There were three men," Nerissa said. "I saw the twins fighting another one of them outside."

"Three is no better," Jarold scoffed.

"It seems they know our disguise but not how many members are in our party," Rian said.

Raysel nodded in agreement. "We need to leave as soon as possible. But first we need to find the printer and ask him again about the book, even though I have a feeling I know what his answer will be."

Rian and Leal led the way out the rear door, checking

warily before stepping outside where the printer, his wife, and his children huddled underneath a large apple tree. The little girl bounded ahead despite her limp to throw herself into the outstretched arms of her mother.

"You signaled those men when we arrived, didn't you?" Raysel accused.

The man's eyes darted between Raysel's face and his sword. "Please don't hurt us. If you punish anyone, then let it be me."

Raysel sighed. "We have no intention to hurt you. We've brought your daughter back safely, haven't we?"

The man wrung his hands anxiously, but he looked slightly relieved. "Yes, those men were sent here weeks ago by King Casimer to await your arrival. They told me to signal them using the watch if anyone ever came asking about books with crystals in their spines. I am a loyal subject of my King. Of course, I would do whatever he and his men asked of me. I already *have* done everything he's asked of me, and yet they threatened to kill us if we didn't cooperate."

"You said you've already done what Casimer has asked. What did you do for him?" Nerissa asked though she had a sinking feeling she knew what his answer would be.

"King Casimer sent out a summons weeks ago to all the printing houses in Marise requesting any and all books with crystals in their spines be brought to him. We had one that was a family heirloom, so we took it to the capital right away. Those men came back with us and have been keeping watch ever since."

The man's words rang out in Nerissa's mind so loudly

that they drowned out all other thoughts. Casimer had one of the books. Had he found the prophecy hidden inside? Did it give a clue to the whereabouts of another book like Alden's had? If so, Alden and Shae could be in danger. *Charis* could be in danger. Nerissa's throat burned at the thought.

She looked the printer in the eye, but he timidly averted his gaze. "It is good to be loyal to your ruler," she said. "But you should remember who it was that threatened you and who returned your daughter safely. Think about that, and decide whether or not it is wise to be loyal to a man who puts his own interests above the safety of his people."

With that, she led the way back to the wagon with the others close behind. They approached as Cole and Eloc were jogging out from a line of trees. The only evidence remaining from their fight was a crimson stain on the gravel.

"What should we do with the bodies still inside the shop?" Leal asked.

"Leave them. The Senka will know we were here whether we bury them or not," Raysel said. His voice was ragged with restrained anger. "Let his loyal subject deal with them."

Having left the horses' saddles and bridles on, they were readied to depart with lightning speed. Nerissa mounted Alba and gripped the reins tightly to keep them from shaking. What were they going to do about the book Casimer now had in his possession? What if they had now lost a key section of the prophecy? And what if he got to the sixth book before they did?

Rian rode up beside her and held out a canteen of water. "Take a drink. You'll feel better." His blue eyes were fierce, determined. "We're all thinking the same thing, but don't worry. We'll find the last book before Casimer does, no matter what."

He looked around to see if anyone else was paying attention to them, and then he leaned over in the saddle and added in a whisper, "My Phoenix."

LIST OF CHARACTERS

MAY CONTAIN SPOILERS

Nerissa's Family and Friends

Addy—Pan's wife

Charis—Nerissa's best friend

Dallin—Childhood friend of Nerissa

Nerissa–Heiress of Chiyo

Pan—Baker in Niamh

Parlen—Nerissa's father, Bond of Chiyo

Rica—Nerissa's mother, Blood of Chiyo

Tao—Nerissa's mentor, teacher, researcher of crystals and their uses

Casimer's family

Amon—Casimer's nephew

Casimer—King of Marise

Echidna—Queen of Marise

Ladon—Prince of Marise

Ohanzee

Alala—Senka defector that takes refuge in Darnal, friend of Caelan

Aravind—Daughter of Haku and Ebba, apprentice blacksmith

Beadurinc—Personal guardian of Parlen and Rica

Caelan—Senka defector that takes refuge in Darnal, Rian's mother, teacher

Caeneus—Mysterious young man brought to Darnal by Einar

Cattleya—Daughter of Haku and Ebba, jewelry designer

Cole—Disguise specialist, twin of Eloc

Ebba—Wife of Haku, blacksmith

Einar—Nerissa's archery instructor, Chief Guardian

Eloc—Disguise specialist, twin of Cole

Gerda—Wife of Hania

Haku—Chief Preceptor

Hania—Chief Advisor

Harbin—Personal guardian of Parlen and Rica

Ildiko—Wife of Einar, practitioner of medicine

Jarold—Swordsman and hand-to-hand combat specialist

Leal—Swordsman

Raysel—Son of Haku and Ebba, First Swordsman of the
    Ohanzee, Nerissa's personal guardian

Rian—Swordsman, Raysel's best friend

Valter—Personal guardian of Parlen and Rica

Senka

Nils—Chief of the Senka

Others

Akkub—Governor of Silvus

Alden—Governor of Rhea

Argia—Prophetess during the time of King Gared

Barr—Friend of Alden's great-grandfather, rumored to be over
    300 years old

Darci—Daughter of Akkub

Desta—Daughter of Shae

Erik—Village messenger, Ohanzee agent

King Gared—First King of Renatus, united the land after the Fall of Civilization

Gladys—Wife of Erik

Gullintanni—Secret group that defends Renatus under orders of King Gared

Matin—Zada's son, Barr's protégé

Shae—Prophetess, extractor of plant oils

Zada—Barr's caretaker

Lands and Towns

Ameles—Tributary of the Yoshie River forming the extreme eastern border of Rhea

Chiyo—Country ruled by Rica and Parlen

Darnal—Hidden city of the Ohanzee

Kisoji—Village in the Northern Mountains near the border between Marise and Rhea

Marise—Country ruled by Casimer and Echidna

Maze—City in Marise with network of underground canals

Niamh—Capital of Chiyo

Nyx—Capital of Marise

Renatus—Name encompassing all the lands of the world

Rhea—Capital city of the mountain province of Rhea

Silvus—Capital city of the province of Silvus

Warren—City in Marise where a large print shop is located

Yoshie River—River that borders Rhea on three sides

THE PROPHECY

MAY CONTAIN SPOILERS

Section 1:

One day Renatus will be divided into two nations, each equal, but opposite. In the days of this new world, the Destroyer of Peace will assume power. His ambition is to guide the future of the entire land. That fate belongs not to him, but instead to the One that will finish the work that King Gared started.

The Destroyer is a creator by nature, and he fosters prosperity with his skill and vision. His ambition grows to consume him and blinds him to the betrayal perpetrated by those he trusts most. The Destroyer will slay the Peaceful Ruler and claim her throne. In doing so, he will set the events in motion that will ultimately result in both kingdoms becoming nothing more than a memory.

The Destroyer will fulfill his wish to rule Renatus, and even the memory of the Peaceful Ruler will be erased. But there is still One who can alter the course of the future. That person, the One who is no more, the One who has become another, the One who was seen before, the Reflection, will appear from the shadows.

Section 2:

The will of the Reflection is the catalyst that guides the fate of the reborn land. They will not seek revenge, but will instead seek to take back the stolen throne. Though the Reflection does not know it, they were born with the power needed to suspend the Destroyer's actions.

All the while, a Traitor toils unnoticed under the Destroyer's command. The Destroyer will be too caught up pursuing his ambitions to recognize the approaching danger, and no guardian's sword will shield him from it. The Traitor will raise the dead, and they will walk, recognized yet unrecognized, amongst the living.

Section 3:

Sickness will spread in the streets of the Destroyer. Both a curse and a blessing, the Destroyer's modern cures will fail to save the ill. An ancient remedy for fluid in the lungs and fever will succeed where the modern one fails.

To be rid of the walking dead, the heirloom hidden among the leaves must be saved. Combine that which sparks from the flames in the forest with the artifice from the mountain city. He who governs the mountains is a true ally, but beware of the spirit that protects the book hidden in the cave.

Section 4:

Deep in the caves, the inborn talent of the Reflection will draw a spark from the Heart of Fire that will ultimately return an ancient power to the world.

They will journey through the ruins in the mountains to the place where time stands still. Here, the lost suspension technique is still remembered. The Reflection will confront the Destroyer using this technique in order to retake the throne without staining their own hands with blood.

Section 5:

The attempt is ill-fated, however. Entering the presence of the Destroyer will put the Reflection in grave peril, and he will spill their blood a second time.

The Destroyer's reign will be brought to an end by one who bears the dragon's mark, but the sword that pierces his heart will not be wielded in malice. In his absence, the

Revenant will seize the empty throne.

Section 6:

Not yet found.

ABOUT THE AUTHOR

Rachel R. Smith lives near Cincinnati, Ohio with her husband and the cutest dog in the world, Sumo. When not writing, she plots to fill the interior of their home with books and mineral specimens and to cover the exterior with roses. Stay up to date on the series and learn more about Rachel by visiting her blog at http://www.recordsoftheohanzee.com or by following Records of the Ohanzee on Facebook (RecordsOfTheOhanzee) and Instagram (@rachel_r._smith).

WORKS BY RACHEL R. SMITH

Reflection: The Stranger in the Mirror

Reflection: Harbinger of the Phoenix

Reflection: Thorn of the White Rose

Reflection: Dragon's Bane

Revenant: The Undead King
(Records of the Ohanzee Book 5, Forthcoming)